W9-AVP-224

"Everything working okay now?"

Everything was tingling, but she wasn't about to tell him that. "I'm not sure."

"Come here and let me check."

Audrey groaned at the seductive gleam in his eyes. "Don't you ever think about anything else?"

Blake considered the question carefully. "Nope. Not since you turned up. Before that, my mind was entirely on this balloon race."

"You have a fascinating array of seduction techniques, Mr. Marshall. Perhaps we should try marketing them to one of the men's magazines. *101 Ways to Get a Woman into Your Arms.*"

"I'd rather think of some way to keep her there. My technique must need work. You keep running away."

"It should give you no end of satisfaction to know that as long as we're up here, I won't get far."

"Eventually, though, we'll have to land," he said, his expression suddenly sobering. "What happens then, Audrey?"

Sherryl Woods has written more than seventy-five romances and mysteries in the past twenty years. She also operates her own bookstore, Potomac Sunrise, in Colonial Beach, Virginia, where readers from around the country stop by to discuss her favorite topic—books. If you can't visit Sherryl at her store, then be sure to drop her a note at P.O. Box 490326, Key Biscayne, FL 33149 or check out her Web site at www.sherrylwoods.com.

SHERRYL WOODS

Can't Say No

This Time Forever

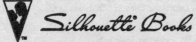

Published by Silhouette Books
America's Publisher of Contemporary Romance

If you purchased this book without a cover you should be aware
that this book is stolen property. It was reported as "unsold and
destroyed" to the publisher, and neither the author nor the
publisher has received any payment for this "stripped book."

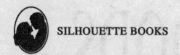 SILHOUETTE BOOKS

ISBN 0-373-80924-7

CAN'T SAY NO

Copyright © 1988 by Sherryl Woods

All rights reserved. Except for use in any review, the reproduction
or utilization of this work in whole or in part in any form by any
electronic, mechanical or other means, now known or hereafter
invented, including xerography, photocopying and recording, or in
any information storage or retrieval system, is forbidden without
the written permission of the editorial office, Silhouette Books,
300 East 42nd Street, New York, NY 10017 U.S.A.

All characters in this book have no existence outside the imagination of
the author and have no relation whatsoever to anyone bearing the same
name or names. They are not even distantly inspired by any individual
known or unknown to the author, and all incidents are pure invention.

This edition published by arrangement with Harlequin Books S.A.

® and TM are trademarks of Harlequin Books S.A., used under license.
Trademarks indicated with ® are registered in the United States Patent
and Trademark Office, the Canadian Trade Marks Office and in other
countries.

Visit Silhouette at www.eHarlequin.com

Printed in U.S.A.

One

"No."

There was a disgusting catch in Audrey's voice. She scowled at herself in the mirror. One simple, common, everyday word and she couldn't get it out with any authority. Ridiculous. She squared her shoulders, lifted her chin defiantly and tried again.

"No!"

This time the word rang out in the tiny motel room. It was firm, emphatic, convincing. Obviously it was not the tone she had used with her boss yesterday, or she wouldn't have been spending the start of her vacation on an assignment that held all the appeal of mud wrestling.

"Audrey, I've got a little problem," Harvey had said on Thursday morning. He'd said it early, before her first cup of coffee, when he knew her resistance was at its lowest.

She had promptly clamped her hands over her ears. "I don't want to hear it. When you have a little problem, it means I have an even bigger one. I'm leaving on vacation in precisely thirty-two hours—" she'd glanced at her watch "—and seventeen minutes. Whatever problems you're having will have to wait until I get back."

"But this won't wait and besides, you're going to love it," Harvey insisted, waving his unlit pipe in her direction and beaming at her. He wore a deceptively jovial look that usually spelled doom. "It's a once-in-a-lifetime opportunity."

Harvey Fielding wasn't known as one of the best public relations men in the country for nothing. He'd joined the Blake Marshall Vineyards when they'd been little more than a field of grapes in the Napa Valley. Now it was one of the fastest-growing California wine companies, thanks to Blake Marshall's genius for business and Harvey's ingenious instincts for promoting it. He was a master at what *Newsweek* had described as "The Hyping of Napa Valley." He'd been one of the first to offer tours of the winery, then gone on to add other enticements for visitors, including a moonlit champagne-and-classical-music concert series that had drawn thousands during the summer months.

Audrey had worked for the company for more than two years. She knew all about Harvey's "once-in-a-lifetime opportunities." The last one had plunked her in a rowboat in the middle of a freezing stream for eight solid hours with a clipboard in her shaking hands and water splashing all over her new sneakers, while a camera crew tried to shoot a thirty-second commercial that Harvey had assured her would be a snap. Not even the presence of one of television's steamiest, most sensual actors had warmed her blood. At least they'd given him hip boots, a sexy brunette actress and a magnum of the finest champagne to hold on to. They hadn't even offered her a sweater. She still couldn't view the ad on television without getting goose bumps.

Harvey was not the steamroller sort of boss. He never made demands. Quite the contrary, he was subtle and persuasive. He knew exactly the right buttons to push—at least with her.

Yesterday morning, for example, his expression had sobered impressively and he'd settled his considerable bulk on the edge of her desk. He'd leaned toward her conspiratorially with that "you're the only one who can handle this" gleam in his eyes, and Audrey automatically had tried to inch her chair out of his line of attack. Unfortunately, she couldn't retreat to the next county fast enough. Besides, Harvey would have followed her. He was looking very determined.

"Look, I know you're supposed to be going on vacation, but I swear I'll make it up to you," he said with enough sincerity to win votes from an opposition party.

"Supposed to be? I *am* going on vacation." Even though she said it firmly, she could still hear the questioning lift in her voice. Damn.

Harvey hurried right on. "It's just one of those things. Joe was supposed to handle this, but his wife—You know Kelly Marie, don't you? A really sweet girl. Anyway, she's expecting a baby...."

There had been this sinking sensation in the pit of Audrey's stomach. She had sighed fatalistically and completed the sentence for him,

"And Joe would never be able to forgive himself, if he weren't around when she delivered."

In retrospect, she knew that was the moment when she should have said no. Emphatically. Instead, thinking of poor Kelly Marie going into labor all alone, she had muttered resignedly, "Okay, Harvey, what's the assignment?"

"The hot air balloon festival in Snowmass." The words sort of ran together in a rush. When Harvey actually displayed overt signs of nervousness, it was definitely ominous.

"What about it?" she asked, eyeing him warily. "Are we providing the champagne? Am I supposed to pour five thousand glasses of our finest?"

Harvey scowled at her sarcasm. "No, it's nothing like that. You won't have to do a thing, really. Just be available. Blake's entered in the race—it's a damn crazy obsession for an executive, if you ask me—but we need one of the PR folks on hand to make sure the media gets anything they need about him or the company. The bio is all prepared. Joe even ran off a history of Blake's record in these ridiculous competitions. Our boss is actually pretty good. He won down in Albuquerque this year and we weren't around to capitalize on it. I don't want that to happen again. All you'll have to do is hand the press the prepared stuff and maybe do one quick release if he wins any of the events this time. I hear one of the networks will be there. You might try to set up something with them." He peeked to check her reaction, then added, "I'd do it myself, but I'm scheduled to work that wine-tasting event in San Francisco."

He tried to make himself sound like a nominee for martyrdom, but Audrey wasn't buying it. She knew all about those wine tastings. Harvey's extraordinary talents would not be taxed. What she didn't know much about were balloon races. She tried to pin Harvey down on the details. "Simple, straightforward PR and that's it? You're absolutely sure? There are no hidden agendas, no arranging middle-of-the-night tête-à-têtes for the boss?"

"From all I've heard, Blake can handle those quite nicely on his own. As for you, you'll get an all-expenses-paid weekend in Snowmass or Aspen. Take your pick. I'll even consider throwing in a few extra days on the company, if you want to spend the rest of your vacation there. I hear it's great in the summer. You can go hiking, go to the music festival, whatever it is people do in those ski resorts when there's no snow on the ground.''

''And my nonrefundable ticket to Hawaii?''

''No problem. We'll cover it and you can reschedule the trip for whenever you like.''

Audrey regarded him warily. There was some little nugget of unpleasant information Harvey had yet to share with her. There had to be. He was still awfully edgy. ''What's the catch?''

''There's no catch.'' He made a little cross-my-heart gesture. Audrey noticed he didn't quite finish it, probably because he knew God would strike him dead on the spot.

''Harvey, I know you. You don't go tossing around paid vacations unless you know there's something I'm going to hate.''

Harvey regarded her indignantly. ''Well, you will be delaying your vacation in Hawaii. I know how much you've been counting on it. Isn't that enough?''

''It is for me, but I have this funny little suspicion nagging at me that it's not enough to explain your sudden burst of generosity. What's the rest?''

''Well, you will have to get up a little early....'' At the lift of her brows, he hurried on, ''But it won't be so bad, really. It's just for a couple of days. You're a real trooper. You can manage.''

"Forget the snow job. How early?"

Harvey stared at the Monet print behind her desk, another ominous sign. Usually he could at least manage to look her in the eyes. Besides, he hated that print. He'd always said it was too "mushy."

"Harvey!"

"You'll have to be at the rodeo grounds in Snowmass by six to keep an eye on what's happening." He beamed at her again… unconvincingly. "But by noon you should have the rest of the day to yourself and it is only for the weekend. After that you can sleep all day, if you want to."

"Six o'clock in the morning?" Audrey had asked in a horrified whisper. "Harvey, you know perfectly well that I can barely get my eyes open by nine. I certainly can't function before that. Do you want to trust Blake Marshall's public relations to a woman who's practically comatose?"

"You won't have to function exactly, at least not at that hour. You just have to show up, look things over, make a few contacts."

"Sounds like functioning to me."

"It'll be a breeze. I promise. You know Blake's reputation. He loves the limelight and the media gravitate to him. He'll do most of his own public relations."

"Then why do I need to be there at all? He'll probably fire both of us, when he discovers you've hired a woman who can't talk in coherent sentences until lunchtime."

"You're doing okay now." Harvey had grinned at her and looked as though he might pat her on the head. If he had, she might very well have slugged him.

Instead, he simply said, "I want you there because Blake Marshall owns this winery. Sales are climbing and he's a hot story, if we play it right. If he wanted the entire public relations staff to fly balloons from Snowmass to the East Coast as a publicity gimmick, we'd all be climbing into those flimsy little baskets."

Even Harvey, who claimed more than his share of unorthodox youthful adventures, had shuddered at that prospect. "Fortunately, he seems to be willing to do that part himself. All you'll need to do is put in an appearance and make sure the press and Blake get exactly what they need, a lot of solid PR for Blake Marshall Vineyards and his *Grapes of Wrath* balloon."

"His what?"

Harvey grimaced. "I know. I didn't pick the name. Ask him about it. Maybe it has something to do with that notorious temper of his."

"I hope it's because he reads Steinbeck," Audrey had retorted, stalking off to make her plane reservations only to discover that Harvey, the smug creep, had already made them for her.

So, here she was on Friday at barely 5:00 a.m., with rain pouring down outside and the temperature hovering around 50 degrees. It was July, for God's sakes! This was definitely not Hawaii.

Three alarm clocks strategically placed around the room and a wake-up call from the front desk were needed just to get her out of bed. She was still standing bleary-eyed in front of a cracked mirror—another ominous sign?—wondering once again why she didn't have any of that noble strength her mother swore her name was supposed to impart. As near as she could recall, the last time she had said no effectively, she had been barely two and it was practically the only word in her vocabulary. According to her parents, it had been her favorite for quite some time. Maybe she'd used it all up.

More likely, she was just a sucker for a sob

story. All that stuff about Joe's pregnant wife, for instance, had gotten to her, played on her sympathy, just as Harvey had known it would. Five minutes after she'd left Harvey, though, she'd realized it was also so much hogwash. Kelly Marie was expecting a baby all right—in October, three months from now. She'd been sitting in her office muttering curses about her gullibility, when Joe had walked in to thank her. He'd looked worried sick.

"Kelly Marie's been having problems," he'd said, running his fingers through his wheat-colored hair. His freckles stood out even more than usual against his pale complexion. "The doctor wants her to stay in bed for the next three months. If she doesn't, we could lose the baby. I just couldn't go away, Audrey. I'm real sorry about your vacation, though. Harvey promised he'd take care of it."

Audrey had immediately forgiven Harvey and thanked heaven that she hadn't given him a rough time about it. It would only have made Joe feel guilty and he didn't need anything more to worry about right now.

"You just take good care of Kelly Marie," she'd reassured him. "I'll work things out with Harvey. Hawaii will still be there, when I get around to it. Is there anything I can do for the two of you before I go?''

''No. Kelly Marie's mom is helping out, too, so we're okay. You just try to have a good time.''

She tried to tell herself that she'd instinctively sensed that Joe's predicament was real, but that was utter nonsense. She'd said yes because being a good sport had gotten to be a habit. Her friends reminded her of that every time she crawled out of bed in the middle of the night to pick one of them up or drove across town in rush hour traffic to substitute for the baby-sitter who'd failed to show up.

Less than a week ago she had been lured into leading an entire troup of raucous Cub Scouts around Fisherman's Wharf, and she still wasn't quite sure how she'd gotten pulled into that! One of her friends had been a very fast talker. Putting her crying, hiccuping eight-year old on the phone to plead with Audrey had probably been the clincher.

''We knew we could count on you'' was rapidly becoming a refrain that turned her stomach.

''Enough is enough,'' she muttered, gesturing determinedly with her toothbrush. ''No more Ms. Nice Guy. No more Understanding Woman.

No more guilt when you turn down some outrageous request. Do you understand that, Audrey?''

"Got it," she retorted sleepily and stepped into the shower. Maybe a week in Aspen wouldn't be so bad after all. Maybe she could use the time to reread every book ever published on assertiveness. Maybe this time their message would sink in and she could go back to California with a new aggressive, stand-firm outlook. It was one thing to be a friend people could call on in a pinch. It was quite another to be a doormat.

By the time she'd made the twenty-minute drive to the Snowmass Village rodeo grounds, she was prepared to say an emphatic no to everything just for practice...with the possible exception of a large cup of very strong coffee.

A half hour later, with caffeine surging through her bloodstream, Audrey stepped gingerly from the shelter where a full-scale country breakfast was being served by volunteers from the Little Red Schoolhouse day care center. The rain had stopped, leaving the cool, damp air smelling crisp and pungent with the lingering scent of horses, though there wasn't a single animal grazing in the sprawling meadow or roaming in the paddock. A sliver of bright blue sky sliced through the dark, low-hanging clouds, hinting that a spectacular dawn was about to break over the snowcapped mountains.

Pickup trucks and cars hauling trailers were pulling into the meadow, where the contestants were beginning to unload their equipment. Cursing the dampness, which was already seeping through her shoes, Audrey headed for the field in search of Blake Marshall.

She'd only met the man once and then very briefly. Yet the impression that remained fixed in her mind was of overwhelming masculinity, self-assurance that bordered on arrogance, and the startling blue eyes and curling dark hair of an Irish rogue. Even if she hadn't seen dozens of newspaper and magazine clippings since then, she doubted she would have any trouble in spotting him. She'd need only to look for the largest circle of beautiful, adoring women dressed in the very latest color-coordinated sportswear, their flowing waves of sun-streaked hair pushed back by designer sunglasses.

As she worked her way toward the launch area, she was suddenly overcome with unexpected curiosity at the bustle of activity around her. She'd never imagined that this many people could be masochistic enough to rise before dawn. She paused as one of the contestants began to unload the cargo from a trailer.

Out came the gondola, which resembled an oversize wicker basket with an identifying number on the side. Then came a huge fan that reminded her of the kind that were once used to cool living rooms in a pre-air-conditioned era, followed by a dangerous-looking propane tank. Finally came a huge bundle of burgundy material. She eyed it skeptically. It didn't look nearly sturdy enough to provide a means of transportation over the mountain range. In fact, it didn't look like something that ought to get off the ground.

"Hey, you! You in the burgundy shirt."

The husky, masculine voice came from about fifty feet away and had an imperious tone that immediately made her hackles rise. She whirled around to encounter the scowling features of Blake Marshall, hands on slender, denim-clad hips, a bright blue windbreaker stretched taut across broad shoulders. Fully prepared to offer some snappy retort, she found herself simply trying to catch her breath. He was far more formidable than she'd remembered and as sexy as the most lurid tabloids had portrayed him.

"You work for me, right?"

"Yes. I'm Audrey Nelson. I work—"

"Never mind all that," he said impatiently. "Just get over here."

Audrey wanted to believe that the man had an incredible memory for the faces of each and every one of his employees. In fact, for an absurd, fleeting instant, she wanted to believe he'd never forgotten their one brief encounter in Harvey's office, but she suspected his recognition had more to do with her burgundy-colored "Marshall Arts" sweatshirt. They'd been given to members of the company softball team. The pun of its name hadn't been the only thing wrong with that team. It had been neither strong, nor particularly adept. The mere fact that she was even on it had been a bad omen. She had reluctantly volunteered, after Harvey had told her that they were desperate—*"really desperate"*—for one more player to substitute in emergencies. He'd spent the first three games patiently trying to explain the rules. Fortunately she'd never had to go to bat.

"You're late," Blake announced as she strode slowly toward him, feeling a sudden surge of adrenaline that had nothing at all to do with the coffee. She wasn't wild about his attitude, but that smoldering look in his eyes was something else. "I wanted the crew here at six."

There was something wrong with that sentence, but she was too sleepy to put her finger on it. "I was here at six. I stopped to get some coffee. Is there something in particular you'd like me to do for you, Mr. Marshall?" She was deliberately cheerful and cooperative. The man was her boss, after all. There was no point in antagonizing him. Harvey had warned her he took this balloon race nonsense seriously. Maybe the media had been bothering him and he was looking for someone to act as a buffer. She wasn't sure she was alert enough to fend off flies, much less a pesky reporter, but she was willing to try.

"You can start by opening the envelope," he said briskly. "John will help you, if you need him." Then he turned his back on her and went back to doing whatever mysterious task he'd been doing before he spotted her.

"I beg your pardon." Maybe this envelope of his contained important instructions, but she didn't see one lying around. Nor did she have the vaguest idea who John was.

He glanced over his shoulder and regarded her quizzically. "You do know how to unroll it, don't you?"

"Not exactly." She still didn't even know what it was, but saw no point in giving away too much about her ignorance. It was bad enough that she was having to delve through mental mush to come up with words that made sense.

Blake shot a disgusted gaze heavenward, then grabbed the balloon—so that's what it was—and began demonstrating. "That's all there is to it. Even a novice should be able to do it. Where the hell did you take your lessons?"

Audrey shot him a horrified look. "But that's not what I'm here for." What if the damn thing got all tangled up and crashed because of something she'd done? She'd be responsible for the death of the man *Fortune* had described as California's brightest young entrepreneur, one of the men to watch in the coming decade. If the courts didn't get her, Harvey surely would. "Wouldn't you rather I go look for some of the media?"

"What do I need with the media? They'll be crawling all over the place once the race is over. Now, let's haul it, woman. We haven't got all morning. We have to get the balloon launched and out of the way, so the next group can get into the area.''

Audrey looked at the dark burgundy bundle, then glanced around at the other workers. A grizzled old man shot her an encouraging, sympathetic smile. Audrey gave him a wobbly grin and shrugged her shoulders. If Blake Marshall wanted to entrust his life to the hands of an amateur, who was she to argue? Surely she could manage a simple task like unrolling this stupid thing.

The old man moved to her side and introduced himself as John Harley. ''Don't mind Blake, missy. He's always a little jumpy before he takes off. Just follow his directions and you'll do just fine. He's one of the best around at this.'' He winked at her. ''But if he gets too pushy, tell him off. Won't hurt him none to be put in his place, especially by a pretty young gal like you.''

''Thanks, I'll remember that.'' It was advice she ought to hang on to. Blake Marshall had a definite arrogant streak that needed taming. Then again, she had no business being the one to try it. ''Could you give me some clue about handling this thing?''

"I'd be happy to, missy."

As Audrey set to work, fumbling over the routine task, Blake's black eyebrows knit together in a puzzled frown. It wasn't like his partner to send him an inexperienced crew member, not for a race as important as this one. Why the hell couldn't he remember the name Cal had given him? Had it been Audrey? The woman had said she worked for him and she was wearing one of the company shirts, so she must be the one. Though he'd caught the tiniest glimmer of fear in her eyes when he'd assigned her the task of opening the envelope, while he went over the propane tanks and gondola.

As he completed his checks, he studied her. She was working gamely at the assigned task, and he noticed that John Harley had gone to her assistance and seemed to be giving her one of his special pep talks. No wonder. She had a helpless, if determined, look about her that appealed to something deep inside him that he'd thought had died long ago. Its sudden reawakening might have convinced him to get to know her better, if he'd met her on any other day.

Not this morning, though. Now he had to focus all his attention on getting the balloon into the air so he could judge the wind direction and speed at several altitudes. The first day's competition was a distance race to Glenwood Springs and he wanted to win it. From the moment he had started ballooning seriously, he'd wanted to be the best. He was closing in on his goal now, but to reach it he needed a support team as skilled and intuitive as he was. This Audrey had better know what she was doing or he'd have Cal's hide.

He shrugged and dismissed his concern as he began the task of hooking the balloon to the gondola, then turning on the fan's generator to begin the slow inflation process. As cold air filled the huge balloon, it unfurled to reveal a graceful trail of grapes winding across the wide expanse as it might along an arbor. *Grapes of Wrath* was written in white, three-foot-high script around the base of the balloon. He had spent nearly twenty thousand dollars for the design and construction, and it still sent a thrill of pleasure through him when it was displayed in all its colorful majesty.

He glanced over and saw the woman was staring at the huge balloon with a spark of excitement in her eyes that hadn't been there when she'd first joined him. With a jolt, it occurred to him that it was the expression of someone who'd never seen a balloon up close before. Dear God, surely that couldn't be.

"What do you think of it?" he asked.

"It's incredible," she said with a satisfying note of awe. He told himself it was the admiration of another enthusiast for a beautifully designed, well-constructed balloon and, though he was still troubled, he dismissed his doubts again.

He couldn't tear his gaze away from her face quite so easily, though.

Wide-eyed, she was glancing around the meadow at the splash of vibrant colors that would soon fill the sky. For the first time, Blake noted the startling violet shade of her eyes, the fringe of thick dark lashes and the gamine face with its pert nose and surprisingly full, sensual lips. They were ripe lips that tempted and lured. He immediately experienced an unexpected and disturbing tightening in his loins. With a sheer effort of will, he determinedly turned his attention to the rest of his ground crew.

"Are we all set?"

"It looks good, boss," John Harley said. "I've been scouting around a little, too, and there ain't no reason I can see why you won't walk away with this one."

"It's not walking I'll be doing," Blake reminded the older man, who'd taught him everything he knew about balloon competition. "We've got to make this baby soar if I'm going to beat Larry Hammond. According to the weather service there should be some terrific air currents. All I have to do is find 'em and then hang on for the ride."

"I wish I weren't too damn old or I'd be up there with you. This old ticker of mine can't take the altitude anymore. Some days I miss it worse 'n not having a woman around."

Audrey listened to the two men talking and caught some of their enthusiasm. For the first time since she'd risen at such an ungodly hour, she felt terrific, even invigorated. It had a lot to do with the day, which had fulfilled its early-morning promise by whisking the last of the clouds away beyond the mountain range. The sun was burning off the morning chill and the azure sky was a postcard-perfect backdrop for the bright yellows, reds, greens and blues that were billowing to the height of tall buildings as they filled with cool air. Her exhilaration also had just a little to do with the man who'd been working side by side with her and John Harley. Blake's instructions had been crisp and precise, but after his initial sternness he'd flashed her a

few unexpected and thoroughly devastating
smiles that had made her pulse skip erratically.

Now he hopped over the edge of the gondola
and began checking the equipment for a second
time, sending a stream of fire upward to heat the
air in the balloon, which tugged against the teth-
ers holding it to the ground. His concentration
was intense, his finely chiseled mouth was set in
a line of determination.

Audrey had never met a man who seemed to
thrive so on what she considered such a frivo-
lous challenge. She'd met ambitious men, who
viewed success as the ultimate achievement with
money as the only measurement. She'd met
womanizers who thrilled only to the chase and
left behind a wake of broken-hearted lovers. She
supposed she'd even met a few men who took
their games—tennis, golf, even poker—seriously. But there was a fierce, single-minded edge
to Blake Marshall's drive to win that was a bit
frightening in its intensity.

It also piqued her curiosity. What made such
a man tick? Why wasn't he satisfied with the
professional acclaim, the growing wealth, the
well-publicized social whirl?

"Are you all set?" he was asking her now,

his voice still rough with an early-morning huskiness that strummed across her nerves.

"Yes. I think I have everything I need."

"Okay, then, why don't you hop in?"

Audrey's delicately arched brows shot up and her mouth dropped open.

"Hop in?" she repeated blankly.

Blake acted as though he hadn't heard the note of horror in her voice or noticed that her complexion was turning an interesting shade of green. "Here, I'll give you a hand."

Before she could voice a violent protest, one exceptionally strong arm snagged her around her waist and the other caught her behind the knees. She felt herself being effortlessly lifted high in the air, then set back on her feet in the confined space of the gondola. She grabbed the sides and started to hoist herself right back out again, but Blake's hand was firmly attached to her belt.

"Whoa! Where do you think you're going?"

With the strength of sheer terror, she jerked free, whirled around and faced Blake Marshall, her eyes flashing with the sparks of a finely cut amethyst. This time she found the words and the emphasis that had been missing in her conversation with Harvey, the authoritative, indignant tone that might have saved her from getting into this preposterous situation in the first place.

"Let me out of here, you idiot! I am not going up in this thing!"

"It's too late to back out now, love. When I hire a crew, I expect them to stay until the job's done," he said. "I want you along for this ride." As if that settled the matter, his attention once more focused entirely on the equipment.

With Blake's attention diverted, Audrey scrambled back toward the side. "I am not one of your crew and it is not too late," she said, trying desperately to swing one leg up over the edge of the basket…gondola…whatever.

If only she'd been half-awake, she would have seen this coming. From the minute he'd put her to work, she would have realized he'd mistaken her for someone else. Well, she'd just have to get out of here and find that someone else for him. Either that or he could fire her. She didn't much care, as long as she stayed on the ground where God had meant her to be.

With a dawning sense of absolute horror, she realized it was too late. The ground was receding rapidly and she felt the gentle, almost indiscernible sway of the basket as it drifted skyward. She looked from the shrinking landscape below to the flames shooting puffs of hot air above her head, then glanced out toward the mountains looming before her in the distance.

"Oh, my God," she sighed softly, clamping her eyes shut and sinking down into a sitting position. She drew her legs up to her chest, wrapped her arms around them and buried her face on her knees. "I will never, ever, not in a million years forgive Harvey for this."

Two

Subconsciously, Audrey's solemn vow registered in Blake's head, and suddenly he really looked at her for the first time. She was huddled in the bottom of the gondola and clinging to her purse with the desperate, white-knuckled grip of a woman trying to prevent a mugging.

An unexpected and untimely shaft of sympathy pierced his heart and he muttered a disgusted oath under his breath. Judging from the way she was swallowing and from her ashen complexion, she was probably trying to quell the beginnings of a well-earned anxiety attack.

Why the devil hadn't he listened to his instincts? From the moment he'd met her, he'd sensed that Audrey Nelson didn't know a blasted thing about ballooning. Hell, she'd told him as much.

But then he'd been lured by something in the depths of those violet eyes of hers and some part of him—no doubt his self-indulgent libido—had wanted her along for the ride almost as much as he'd wanted to win the race. Blake was used to taking risks. He thrived on them, in fact. Hauling Audrey Nelson into the gondola over her protests had been a risk, but one he'd been so certain would pay off.

His well-honed self-confidence had convinced him it just might be possible to have both a victory and the companionship of the woman with the delightfully fiery temper, valiant determination and, most intriguing of all, an almost childlike sense of wonder. With some arrogantly masculine, possessive urge, he'd wanted to initiate her into the glories of ballooning and he'd simply made up his mind to do it. That same decisiveness had made him a success at business, but today it just might have gotten out of hand. If only he hadn't felt such an unexpected and overwhelming need to hear that tart tongue of hers whispering his name, he might have stopped to think twice about what he was doing.

What an insensitive fool he'd been!

For one thing, he hadn't counted on her sheer terror. For all of Audrey's rather vocal protests, he'd expected eventual delight and he was still getting unfeigned panic. Obviously more than inexperience was at play here. He had to find some way to distract her, to calm her down before she fainted. He'd have enough trouble guiding the balloon without having her passed out at his feet or delivering well-aimed blows to his shins, which was what he suspected she wanted to do.

Charm, Marshall, all the tabloids say you have it.

Almost casually, he glanced down at her. Referring to her muttered threat—the last words she'd spoken—he asked, "Harvey who?"

He already suspected the answer, and he knew now why there'd been a sense of familiarity about Audrey, the allure of some elusive past connection. Obviously, he'd seen her around the office.

Blake didn't spend a lot of time in the corporate office. He preferred the action of the fields or processing plant. The men and women who worked the fields had led tough, migratory lives until he'd given them a feeling of permanence. They worked hard with a sense of pride and dignity that he admired and respected. The men who took the grapes and turned them into wine were craftsmen. They excelled at the challenge of creating the best in a highly competitive field. Again, he found them more fascinating than the corporate desk jockeys he'd met through the years.

Spending as little time behind his own desk as he did, it was no wonder he was only beginning to suspect what Audrey's real role was at Blake Marshall Vineyards. If she worked for Harvey, she had to be tough and competent. Like him, Harvey wouldn't tolerate anyone who couldn't pull her own weight.

"Harvey Fielding," she responded. She scowled at him fiercely as she uttered the name with the vehemence of a curse. At least it had brought the color back into her cheeks. "You'd better start looking for a new PR executive, because when I get my hands on him I intend to do serious bodily damage to him."

He fought to suppress a smile. She was maybe 110 pounds to Harvey's 225. It ought to be an interesting battle. "Harvey's a good man. I don't suppose you could leave him in one piece? Maybe if you'd just relax and enjoy the ride?" he suggested hopefully.

"Not even for a hundred exorbitantly expensive bottles of your well-publicized private stock of cabernet sauvignon," she retorted without so much as an instant's hesitation. She was one very angry lady. In this mood, she just might be able to take Harvey on.

Blake winced. "I'm almost afraid to ask, but do you know anything at all about ballooning, or is this a first trip?"

"Do I look like I do this every day?" Audrey snapped back. "I'm not exactly convinced about the aerodynamics of a plane. This flimsy contraption isn't even in the same league. Now that you know the awful truth about me, you can put this thing down anytime and I'll be out of your way."

It was a sensible suggestion. It was certainly the only way he was likely to win the race to Glenwood Springs. He couldn't concentrate on piloting and on her at the same time. Then his eyes roved leisurely over her, darkening appreciatively as they lingered on the full breasts heaving beneath her baggy sweatshirt. His heart pounded in a way he hadn't experienced in a

very long time. It was a fine time for it to engage
in acrobatics. He took a very deep breath, then
made his decision.

"I don't think so," he said slowly.

Audrey swallowed hard, but managed a con-
fident, direct stare that increased his admiration
for her. She was definitely a gutsy spitfire. She
might be scared out of her wits, but she wasn't
one whit intimidated—or fascinated—by him. It
was a unique experience. Most women, especially those who were interested in his sizable
bank account, went out of their way to be ac-
commodating. They'd have declared a passionate shared interest in ballooning. Some of them
actually seemed to think if they got him at a high
enough altitude, he'd lose his senses and pro-
pose.

Unlike those women, Audrey Nelson de-
pended on him for a paycheck, yet she was more
than willing to tell him to take a flying leap
straight out of this balloon. And she was definitely not harboring any thoughts of marriage.
In fact, she was staring at him right now as
though he were a particularly repulsive, if somewhat intriguing creature.

"Why on earth not?" she asked incredulously. "I thought you wanted to win this race.

Harvey says you've got this absurd obsession about winning and after listening to you issue orders down there like a drill sergeant, I have to agree with him. You're a little weird on the subject.''

She regarded him speculatively. ''It's not too late, you know. Most of the others probably aren't even ready to take off yet. You have plenty of time to find the qualified person this Cal sent. I'll just get busy on those press releases. We'll forget this little incident ever took place.''

She gave him what she obviously hoped would be a persuasive smile. He grinned back. All that good humor—hers so clearly phony, his sincere—hung in the air.

''Do you intend to let Harvey forget?''

Her smile faded so rapidly it made him regret having brought up the subject. ''Perhaps sometime in the next fifty years or so,'' she said darkly. ''Until then, I want him to pay dearly for getting me into this.''

''Harvey didn't get you into this,'' he reminded her. ''He sent you to Colorado on a perfectly legitimate PR assignment. I hauled you into the balloon. Are you going to make me pay as well?''

Her icy gaze met his, challenged the fiery look in his eyes, then faltered. The ice melted. "I've already said we could drop it, if you'll just get me back on the ground." It was a plea of sorts, but she was trying very hard not to beg. He liked that, too.

"I have plenty of work to do down there," she added, when he didn't respond. "There are probably newspaper people, maybe even magazine writers from all over. We could get terrific coverage. I think I even saw a network camera crew. Harvey especially wanted me to try to set something up with them. If he doesn't see you on the national news tonight, he'll have my hide."

Blake waved his hand dismissively. "Forget the releases. The press has enough background and gossip about me to fill the entire feature section."

Her hard-won control snapped then and her eyes flashed at him angrily. "Then why the hell did you want someone from public relations out here?"

He shrugged. "You know Harvey. When he told me about Joe's situation, I told him it wasn't necessary, that I'd handle things myself, but the man takes his job seriously. He seems to think if he has someone around, I'll stay in line.''

Suddenly, Audrey laughed. It began as a chuckle low in her throat. The sound rippled sensuously along his nerves, before erupting into a full-scale roar. Tears rolled down her cheeks. He watched her anxiously.

"Are you okay? You aren't going to go hysterical on me, are you?"

The laughter died and she shot him a calculating look. "Will it get me down?"

"Probably not."

She choked back another nervous laugh, rubbed the tears from her cheeks and sighed. "Then I won't waste my energy."

She studied him curiously, and Blake felt another wave of heat sear his insides. "I'm surprised at Harvey," she said, when she'd completed her rather thorough, disconcerting examination. "He's usually very perceptive, but you don't strike me as the type of man who's easily kept in line. Goodness knows, I'm not having any luck at it."

"Maybe you're not trying hard enough."

A flush stained her cheeks as she caught the blatant innuendo, but she responded gamely,

"Does Harvey have some special technique he failed to share with me?"

"Nope, but he does keep trying. I used to think he was worried about me, but then I figured out it was only the company. Every time my picture turns up on a tabloid at the supermarket checkout, he's convinced our sales will plummet."

"If you ask me, they'd probably go up. The same people who read those things for vicarious thrills will probably buy your wine just to see if it improves things for them the way it has for you. Do you realize there are probably thousands of men sipping your Chablis and expecting some incredibly sexy actress to materialize by their side?"

Blake grinned at her. "Precisely my point. The company benefits from my image. It was a calculated intention on my part that began the day I took over a failing winery and swore to turn it around. It's probably the only PR gimmick for which Harvey isn't responsible. Now I'm caught in my own trap. If I had my way, I'd live a quiet, secluded life-style, surrounded by five or six kids and a doting wife."

She regarded him skeptically. "Why don't you, then? According to the figures I put in the annual report, the company is now on solid financial ground. Surely, you no longer have to make the supreme sacrifice of dating all those gorgeous women just to keep it afloat." She sounded as though she found the thought of all those women intensely irritating. "Maybe you're enjoying it more than you want to admit."

To his astonishment, he realized that her irritation pleased him. Normally he sent a woman packing at the first sign of jealousy. Instead, he found himself wanting to offer some explanation that would remove that disdainful look from her eyes. She'd obviously accepted his playboy reputation as fact and found it distasteful. He wondered if she'd believe the truth coming from him, especially when he was holding her hostage. He decided to try.

"Actually, my exploits have been greatly exaggerated. These days I'd be a fool if I behaved as irresponsibly as the press would like everyone to believe I do. Even so, doting wives are hard to come by in my particular circle of so-called friends, especially if it means living on a ranch that doesn't even offer a Jacuzzi. Most of the women I know can't live that far from Saks and Neiman-Marcus, much less Elizabeth Arden and their personal fitness trainer. Not one of them has any desire to see a grape until it's been duly processed into an expensive vintage of wine.''

Suddenly he peered at her intently. ''Let me see your nails.''

A dark brow lifted quizzically. ''My nails? Aside from a tendency toward kidnapping, you also have some weird thing about fingernails?''

He grinned. Thank God, she was finally making jokes. He tapped her on the nose. ''Just humor me. Hold out your hands.''

Like a child whose hand-washing technique was being evaluated by a critical parent, she glowered at him, but she held out her hands for his inspection. They were dainty, the sort of hands that could caress a man with a gentle, magical touch. Her short nails, just long enough for setting up shock waves along a man's spine, were buffed to a clear shine.

''I knew it,'' he said approvingly, sharply aware of the little frisson of excitement that was racing along his own spine. ''You don't spend half your life at a manicurist. Do you realize how many women go into a deep depression if they break a nail? Do you realize how often some of them change their polish to match their outfits? I've been left cooling my heels while some woman had her nails wrapped, whatever that is,'' he muttered in bewilderment. Sometimes he wondered how he'd survived the inanity of it.

"Sounds like a tough life,'' Audrey said with a touch of mockery. If he'd been expecting sympathy, he'd definitely taken the wrong tack. She gestured at the balloon. "What about this? Where does this fit in? Are all the stories about your obsession with this exaggerated, too? Is this just another public relations ploy?''

Audrey watched closely as Blake's blue eyes instantly sparkled with unsophisticated, boyish excitement. She saw the tension leave his shoulders and the gentle softening of his lips. "Now this is something else again,'' he said in that husky tone that played over her nerves like a lover's caress. "Every word you've ever read about my love affair with this is probably true.''

"I don't get it. Is it the danger, the thrill, what?''

"It's an escape. It gives me a sense of total freedom, a release from all the pressures of work, even though it has its own challenges. I think all of us harbor a desire to be able to experience flight like a bird. This is the closest man can come.''

"It's a little too close, if you ask me."

"Come on now," he chided. "Just take a look around."

"I'd rather not," she muttered, pointedly keeping her gaze directed at his knees, where the denim of his jeans was unexpectedly and charmingly worn and faded. Good heavens, what was wrong with her? She didn't want to be charmed by anything about this man—not his infectious smile, his brief flashes of sensitivity and certainly not by a worn spot in his pants. "I think I'll just stay right down here. I get dizzy standing on the first step of a ladder."

"Come on," he taunted persuasively. "You're no coward."

"Who says?"

"I do. Stand up. You don't know what you're missing." He held out his hand. His fingers were square and strong, his hands roughened by work, good honest labor. Blake Marshall was clearly no pampered executive and, for all the publicity, he was apparently far more than a jet-setting playboy. She'd heard tales of his days in the fields working side by side with his men. She'd thought they were merely publicity schemes dreamed up by Harvey. Now she saw the proof. It only added to the enigma.

When Audrey took his hand at last, she told herself she wasn't abandoning her fury at her predicament, that she wasn't giving in. Except, perhaps, to temptation. She allowed him to pull her to her feet, then didn't do a thing to stop him when he drew her to his side. She told herself she needed the support, especially since her eyes were clamped tightly shut again.

"Now just look around," he urged. "Have you ever seen anything any more beautiful?"

She opened one eye and peeked. A bright yellow balloon, decorated with a large rat that reminded her rather vividly of her opinion of Harvey, hovered a few hundred feet away. A multicolored balloon was just above them to the right. Snowcapped mountain peaks beckoned from a distance, and far, very far, below were thousands of colorful specks dotting the meadow like so many wildflowers.

"People?" she mumbled in a choked whisper. "Those are people down there? Exactly how high up are we?"

"Not so far."

"How high, Blake?"

"Maybe a thousand feet, probably less. That's nothing. We're just drifting now. Wait until we go over the mountains."

She twisted around until she could get a good look at his face. He seemed to be serious.

"I am not going over any mountains," she said adamantly. An assertive woman made her point without wavering, wasn't that what she'd read? "Am I making myself clear? No way. You do not pay me enough money to make me go one foot higher in this thing."

The blasted man grinned at her. "Perhaps not," he said, "but I do seem to have you at a disadvantage, unless you brought along a parachute."

She obviously didn't have the knack quite yet for making herself perfectly clear. He thought she was still pussyfooting around. Like Harvey, he was just hunting for the right buttons to push. In this case, there most definitely weren't any. She wanted to be back on the ground and she wanted to be there now! She was tired of being understanding about this little case of mistaken identity. She was tired of being patient. And she was definitely tired of floating around up here, like a dandelion caught on a breeze. The only thing she wasn't tired of was Blake and that wasn't something she cared to deal with.

"Blake Marshall, you take me back down there this instant or I will report you to every government agency I can think of that supports and enforces employee rights. I will charge you with harassment, unsafe working conditions, discrimination. I will dream up so many lawsuits, your attorneys will be able to retire on what you'll have to spend to defend yourself.''

Her outburst, of which she was particularly proud, didn't seem to faze him one whit. ''Harassment, huh? Sexual harassment? An interesting idea.''

There was a decidedly wicked gleam in his eyes that suddenly made her even more nervous. Her heart, which had been ready to stop when she looked out and saw where she was, was now palpitating so fast she was sure she ought to be heading straight for an emergency room. She doubted if Blake would even bother to call Mountain Rescue. His mind seemed to be on other things. Her mouth, for instance. He seemed to find it fascinating.

His arm, which had never loosened its firm grip on her waist, tightened just a bit and his head lowered ever so slowly. She could see the kiss coming, could feel the warm whisper of his mint-scented morning breath against her cheek and she was powerless to stop it. Blast it all, she didn't even want to, which was the worst trick yet this morning. What good did it do to say no, when your whole body was shouting yes? Blake was a perceptive man. He obviously heard those shouts all too clearly.

She caught the triumphant gleam in his eyes just before his lips covered hers, slanting heat across trembling moistness. She had just a fraction of a second in which she might have managed a half-hearted objection, but it stuck in her throat as his mouth teased gently and then possessed, taking away not only her breath, but all thoughts of protest. In fact, there wasn't a rational thought left in her head as she gave herself up to the most provocative, enticing sensations she'd ever experienced.

Maybe it was the altitude. More likely, it was Blake Marshall teaming up with her suddenly rampaging hormones. Whatever it was, the kiss left her weak and chastened and just about willing to do anything the man suggested, short of jumping out of the gondola at one thousand dead-on-crashing feet. For a woman who'd planned to spend the next week learning to be assertive, it was obvious she'd failed the first lesson. Worse, with Blake's arms tight around her, she didn't even mind.

Then the phrase ''good sport'' crept into her

mind, followed by "understanding woman." It was like hearing a battle cry, with enemy troops just over the crest of a hill. She put her hands against Blake's rather solid chest and shoved with all her might.

"You have some nerve!" she said indignantly, when she could manage to get a word out without sounding all breathless and fluttery. "Is this how you seduce your string of women? Do you get them up in one of these dumb balloons and then take advantage of them, when they don't have anyplace to run?"

"At the risk of sounding egotistical, most women I know aren't interested in running."

"Well, I am. I don't even know you. I do not go around kissing strangers."

"Then I guess we'll just have to change that, won't we?" he said with absolute calm as he shot another blast of hot air into the balloon.

Audrey had seen enough by now to know that the hot air sent them up, not down. Her stomach rolled over. "Change what?" she asked, regarding him warily.

"The fact that we're strangers."

Audrey didn't want to be disagreeable, not if it would end her captivity at a height that made her head swim. "Fine. We'll meet later for drinks. After the race. A friend told me about this great little outdoor café in Aspen. We can have a drink and celebrate your victory.''

"Why wait?"

Good question. He'd already heard most of her salient answers and he wasn't particularly impressed with them. She tried one last time to remind him of the race. Not so long ago it had been all-important.

"How much talking will we be able to do, if you have to keep your mind on the race?"

One brow arched. "You could help. Working side by side often makes a relationship much stronger."

She folded her arms stubbornly across her chest. "Not on your life."

"Then I can probably manage to do two things at once." His glance slid over her with provocative slowness. His voice softened to a purr. A little more oomph and it would have been a predatory growl. "If I couldn't and had to choose, though, I think I'd opt for getting to know you."

Her pulse leaped crazily.

Flattery, Audrey, that's all it is, she told herself. A man resorts to insincere flattery when he's losing his case. All she had to do was mus-

ter a few more convincing arguments along this
line and she'd be down on the ground in no time
and Blake would be soaring on to another victory. Harvey would have his publicity coup and
she would have her sanity, to say nothing of
keeping her limbs in one piece.

Then, Blake lifted his gaze to meet hers and
her optimism faded, along with rational thought.
There was a depth of sincerity in his eyes that
rattled her more than anything else that had happened all morning. Her mouth dropped open in
astonishment, then her heart began to pound.

Oh, sweet heaven! she thought, her eyes wid-
ening in dismay.

There was absolutely nothing more disconcerting than a man who switched obsessions
when you were least expecting it. She had the
oddest feeling that she wouldn't feel one bit
more panicky, if he'd suddenly announced that
the bottom was about to drop out of the gondola.

In fact, she was beginning to think that was
the only way she was ever likely to get back
down to earth.

little announcement made her blood run cold. She'd been arguing with Blake for the better part of an hour to no avail. Five minutes didn't seem like nearly long enough to come up with a clincher.

The announcer went on with what she thought was disgusting enthusiasm. "Today's event is an unusual one, a long distance race, with the winner being determined by the distance achieved. For those of you who plan to follow on the highway, keep an eye on that blue and gold balloon piloted by Larry Hammond of Austin, Texas, and on the *Grapes of Wrath*, piloted by Blake Marshall, who makes that excellent California champagne you're all sipping today."

Nice PR, Audrey thought instinctively, then wondered about the announcement's overall implications for her under the current circumstances. She didn't have to wonder for long.

"Word has it these two men have been locked in a fierce competition on the circuit this year. Right now, they're tied. This weekend's three events will break the deadlock, so you can bet they're going to give us a hell of a race."

Audrey's startled gaze shot to Blake's face and caught the grim expression as he surveyed Larry Hammond's balloon. Unexpected sympathy welled up and replaced both her irritation and her single-minded concern about her own safety.

"This race isn't just for fun," she said. "It's much more important to you than you've been admitting, isn't it?"

Blake refused to meet her eyes. "I've been after Larry Hammond for the past five years, practically since the day I started ballooning. This year I've finally caught him," he said in a neutral tone.

Despite his apparent indifference, she could see the tension in his shoulders. She also thought she could sense his disappointment. He had to know he was giving up his shot at a victory by keeping her with him.

"Then why on earth don't you give yourself a real chance? Get someone up here who knows what they're doing."

Blake shifted uncomfortably, but he didn't respond. They were hovering just a short distance above the ground now, too high for Audrey to jump, but low enough for her to seriously consider it. She could see John Harley and the rest of Blake's ground crew waving frantically and pointing at a man in their midst, who was obviously supposed to be where she was. Despite the sparks between her and Blake, and because of those fiery dragon's flames shooting above her head, she would have gladly traded places with him.

She caught a flicker of temptation in Blake's eyes, but it vanished almost as quickly as it had come. He gave her a jaunty grin. "I think the two of us can do it."

"Blake!" She uttered his name with an exasperated moan. "What on earth is with you? You're certainly not being very practical. Unless having me around for ballast is a help, I won't be of much use to you."

"If you work for Harvey, then you know how to take directions. I know what a stickler for details he is."

"Harvey knows my limitations. He has never asked me to fly a balloon before," she pointed out. "He's stuck with the simple stuff like writing press releases and pulling together the annual report. The most daring thing he's ever asked me to do was to choose the ink for the company stationery. Even then, he was very nervous until he saw that I hadn't picked orange."

"Just think of the absolutely fascinating, realistic press release you'll be able to write, after you experience this firsthand."

"Part of the joy of being a writer is that I get to use my imagination," Audrey countered.

Blake parried right back, not with words, but rather with a thoroughly bewitching smile. His lips curved into soft temptation. His eyes dared her. And all of her polite, sensible arguments promptly stuck in her throat.

"Please," he said, his voice thick with husky persuasion. "Won't you just give it a try? For me? I promise you'll be safe. The last thing I'd ever want to do would be to put your life at risk."

For the first time since this crazy odyssey had begun, he actually appeared to be giving her a choice. Yes or no, it was as simple—and as complex—as that. Could she say no to him? Could she turn down a man who was willing to sacrifice a dream just to keep her at his side? Could she break with twenty-seven years of tradition as a good sport?

The last one brought her up short. *A good sport?* She was back to that again. Her head screamed at her to take a stance this time, to say no just this once to prove she could do it, to say it forcefully without wavering. Then she met Blake's hopeful gaze and caught his enticing half-smile.

"Well?" he said softly.

She looked determinedly at the ground below, at the mountains ahead, and tried to give her intellect—and her nervousness—full rein, but her heart was clamoring for equal attention. For some utterly insane reason, it seemed to want to stay up here with a man who had absolutely no scruples. She'd never realized she had a latent suicidal streak, to say nothing of incredibly bad taste in men. Blake might be considered quite a catch by most women, but by her standards he was no better than a presumptuous rake.

"What the hell," she muttered at last. "Let's give it a shot."

As soon as the words were out of her mouth, she groaned, turned away and pounded on the side of the gondola. The willow ridges cut into the soft side of her fist. The pain was almost welcome.

"Poking a hole in this isn't a particularly good idea," Blake said casually. "Care to explain why you feel the need to try?"

She peered over at him. "You'd never in a million years understand."

"As soon as we get this thing moving, why don't you try to tell me? I'm a pretty good listener."

The last thing Audrey wanted to do was inform a man who clearly had a will of iron that she had a backbone with all the resilience of overcooked spaghetti. If he was around her for long, he'd figure it out for himself, a prospect that didn't please her. In fact, it had occurred to her more than once this morning that while she might be increasingly attracted to Blake, he was absolutely the last man on earth she should ever consider looking at twice.

She'd once been involved with a man exactly like him, a man who wouldn't take no for an answer, a man so compelling and strong that her own personality had been swallowed up and lost. Blake was just as overwhelming, and because of that, he was a danger to every vow she'd made to get control of her life, to exchange roller-coaster excitement for serenity. Admittedly, she thought wryly, vows of poverty and chastity probably had a better chance for success in this day and age.

She'd thought she was doing better. While she might still be a pushover for Harvey's requests, at least she put up a halfhearted fight. She only acceded to her friends' desperate calls for help out of long-standing loyalty.

By contrast, she'd just given in to Blake, a

man she'd known less than two hours, with barely more than a whimper of protest. There was no loyalty involved. That wickedly dazzling smile of his, combined with just a hint of vulnerability accompanying his plea, had done it. He'd charmed her into sticking with him. Without even trying very hard, he had overcome every bit of her common sense and outright panic. Who knew what he could talk her into, if he really put his mind to it. She'd probably never say no again.

There was no choice, really. She wouldn't back out now and add indecisiveness to her list of failings, but once this race was over and she had her feet firmly on the ground again, she'd put them to good use...running as far from Blake Marshall as she could, while she still had the will to do it.

"Blake?" John Harley's voice crackled from the hand-held radio that was lying on top of a small cooler. It was one of two radios in the gondola. The other one spewed forth frequent information from the airport tower about aircraft in the vicinity. Audrey had been trying very hard not to think about the implications of that.

"Blake, pick up the radio."

Blake seemed intent on ignoring it.

"Dammit, son, are you out of your mind? Jenkins is down here waiting."

Blake picked up the radio at last, avoiding Audrey's curious gaze. "Sorry. I already have a passenger."

"That little girl looks scared to death. Jenkins paid a fortune for the privilege of being up there with you today. You don't leave a sponsor hanging around on the ground, while you go for some damn joyride."

"This is no joyride. I have every intention of winning. Jenkins will have to be satisfied with that."

"You can't win if your mind's on other things. What happens if something goes wrong?"

"Nothing is going to go wrong. Besides, you'll be following along in the chase truck. I'm sure you won't let us out of your sight."

Audrey was listening to the exchange with a resurgence of her initial panic. If John Harley was concerned about her inexperience, then she was in far more trouble than she realized. She'd gotten caught up in some temporarily romantic notion that floating around up here like a bird was a piece of cake.

"What's he talking about?" she asked Blake. "What kind of trouble?"

"Don't worry about it," he soothed. For a man who'd glibly talked her into going along for the ride, he seemed surprisingly bereft of convincing words just now. "You'll be able to handle anything that comes up."

The reassuring tone was nice, but not nearly enough. "I want to worry about it. I like to worry, especially if imminent death is the subject."

Blake's expression was excessively tolerant. "We are not going to be killed. John was just born cautious."

"Not altogether a bad trait."

"Don't pay any attention to him."

John, however, didn't seem inclined to be ignored. The radio spewed out another stream of static, along with a stern lecture on foolhardiness.

Blake glowered over the side of the gondola and inquired via radio, "Has there been any change in the reports from the weather service?"

Audrey peered down to see John's reaction to having his advice so calmly discounted. He was scowling up at the two of them, his wrinkled face totally disapproving.

"Missy, are you okay?"

Before Audrey could speak for herself, Blake said, "She's fine. Now, what about the weather?"

John muttered something unintelligible, then sighed. "The weather report is unchanged, clear until noon or so, then some storms brewing."

"Thanks, John. We'll see you in Glenwood Springs."

"You do remember where it is, don't you?"

Blake laughed and gave him a thumbs-up gesture. "I checked the map, old man."

"Glad to hear it. You ain't shown much sense about anything else this morning."

"Stop hounding me and get out on the road. If I lose sight of Hammond, keep me posted on his progress."

"If you lose sight of Hammond, you'll have more to worry about than his progress. Over."

"What did he mean by that?" Audrey asked, instantly alert.

"Just that the course should be pretty straightforward. If I can't see Hammond, one of us has gone astray."

"Can that happen?"

"It's possible."

Audrey stared at him and sank back down again. "Oh, my God."

"Don't give up on me now. We've got work to do, woman."

"I'd like an explanation first. Exactly how do we go off course? Don't you know how to steer this thing?"

"Sure," he said confidently. "Up and down."

Her eyes widened. "Up and down? What about forward and back?"

"That's a little trickier."

"How tricky?"

"Actually that part's up to the air currents."

That vague sense of alarm that foolishly had gone into hiding came back with a vengeance. "We're floating around up here at the whim of some fickle wind?"

"In a manner of speaking."

"I've changed my mind. I'd like to take the down ride now."

"Too late, sweetheart. We're off."

Tension made her numb, except for the pulse in her neck that seemed to be fluttering excessively fast. A little more reassurance now would have been nice, but Blake seemed to be occupied with a number of inexplicable maneuvers, including spilling little drops of water over the side of the gondola.

"If that's our water supply, would you mind preserving it?" she requested over the lump that had lodged in her throat. She was beginning to envision spending the rest of the summer and then a long, very cold winter stranded on a mountain with only Blake for warmth. To her disgust, certain aspects of the image held a very strong appeal.

"Just checking the wind. We'll have plenty left if we need it." He opened the vent in the side of the balloon, allowing the air to cool slightly, and guided it down into a more favorable current. His movements were efficient and, even to her untrained eye, skilled. They also displayed his masculine strength to full advantage. He had stripped off his windbreaker and was working in a snug-fitting polo shirt. A thorough exploration of the corded muscles in his arms distracted her temporarily. Those titillating images danced through her head again.

He glanced down at her. "How are you enjoying the ride so far?"

Audrey tried to concentrate on the warmth in his eyes, but she couldn't help noticing that a few remaining, low-hanging clouds were zipping past at a dizzying speed. "I'll let you know later."

Blake stopped what he was doing and gazed at her with concern. "You aren't still afraid, are you?"

"Does the phrase 'stark terror' mean anything to you?"

He knelt down beside her. As a distraction, it was very effective. The bulging muscles of his thighs were mere inches from her fingers. She tried to recall everything she'd ever read in her high school chemistry and biology books, but she couldn't think of a single thing to explain the powerful reaction sweeping over her. It was probably in the sex education text, anyway, and that had been banned from her school.

His hand curved along her jaw and he tilted her head up until their eyes clashed. "You are safe with me," he said gently. "Promise."

Audrey shook her head. Even if he wasn't aware of it, she knew it was a lie. She might be safe enough in this flimsy balloon, though she had her doubts, but she wasn't safe with Blake Marshall at all. She'd have been more secure in a pit of vipers.

"Who's Jenkins?" she asked, just to get her

mind off the urgent and nearly irresistible desire to check out the muscle tone in Blake's thigh.

"A sponsor," he answered and quickly got to his feet. Too quickly. Suddenly he didn't seem interested in meeting her gaze. He couldn't have done more to arouse her curiosity if he'd tried.

"What does that mean?"

"He puts up a chunk of money for these races."

"And he was supposed to fly with you this morning?"

He looked decidedly uncomfortable. "Yeah, well, we'd talked about it," he mumbled, as he pointedly went back to fiddling with more gadgets.

"Is he also a pilot?"

"No."

With a sudden and not especially pleasing flash of insight, Audrey sensed a shift in the balance of power in this conversation. "If he wasn't going to crew for you, then who was?"

"No one." A middle-of-the-night intimacy couldn't have been murmured any more quietly. The impact, however, was decidedly different.

"No one?" she repeated in an ominous tone. "I thought you mistook me for your crew."

"I did."

"Look me in the eye and say that."

"I did." Blue eyes glanced defiantly in her direction, then shifted away. "Sort of."

"Explain."

"Cal was supposed to send someone new for the ground crew."

"Ground being the operative word, I assume."

"Yes, dammit." The guilt-ridden words were ground out between tight lips.

"I see." She nodded thoughtfully. "I hope you don't think I'm being unreasonable, but do you mind my asking what the hell I'm doing here?" Her voice rose until she was sure her shout could be heard three states away.

A tiny muscle worked in Blake's jaw. For the first time since they'd taken off, he was the one who appeared nervous. If she had her way, the man would be quaking in his boots before she finished with him. He would be seeing visions of a long jail term or, at the very least, a hefty fine.

Since it was difficult to be thoroughly intimidating while seated, she got to her feet. Blake still towered over her by several inches, so it wasn't quite as effective as she might have liked, but it was a start. Hands on hips, she glowered at him. "Well?"

He met her gaze and she caught a twinkle in his eyes, before he carefully—and wisely—banished it. She was in no mood to provide him with another second of his morning's entertainment.

"I wanted you along," he finally responded. The simple words set up a thrumming in the air that affected every nerve in her body. She searched the depths of his eyes for any sign of an easy lie, but she couldn't find it. She found sincerity and warmth and, most unexpected of all, desire. Sharp, primitive, unmistakable desire. Her breath caught in her throat.

"Not as crew?" she managed to ask in a raw-edged whisper.

"Not as crew," he confirmed, then admitted with obvious reluctance, "we almost never take crew along on these events."

She allowed her mind to digest that little piece of information.

"I could file kidnapping charges," she said almost casually, glancing at him out of the corner of her eye. He was leaning back against the side of the gondola now and he no longer looked nearly as tense. He was supposed to be quaking by now. Where had she gone wrong? It must have been in the phrasing. She should have sounded more sure of herself, more definite. "In fact, I think I will file them. The minute we get back on the ground, I'll call the FBI or whoever's in charge of those things and file criminal charges."

"Harvey will hate it," Blake pointed out, as if what Harvey thought mattered. If she could think of charges, she'd file them against him, too.

"It'll be really bad PR," he added.

She refused to be daunted by such flimsy, veiled threats. "You should have thought of that before you got me up here under false pretenses."

He took a step toward her. A couple more of those long, easy strides of his would put him very, very close. A wayward shiver of anticipation shot up her spine. When it reached her brain, she gave it a stern lecture, then tried to ignore it.

"Why do I have the feeling that this argument has very little to do with kidnapping?" he said softly.

Her heart fluttered. Her brain told her to ignore that, too. "Why would you say that?"

"For one thing, you agreed to come along with me, so kidnapping's out."

"You can't prove it."

He grinned at her, which was very irritating, and took another step. "You certainly didn't try to get away when you had the chance. I think John will vouch for that. We're up to two against one and I do have something of a national reputation."

His breath whispered past her cheek and left it flushed. She tried to take a step backward, but there was no place to go. She swallowed deeply, then said with as much disdain as she could muster, "Sure, as a rogue. How much good do you think that will do you?"

"I was referring to my reputation in the business world."

"I think that other, carefully cultivated image is the one they'll look at in this instance...man about town, jet-setting playboy, most eligible bachelor, you know the one. Yes, indeed, I don't think a judge would overlook that." She began to inch sideways, trying not to be too obvious about it.

"Tell me something, Audrey. Why do I get the feeling that what we're battling about here is control? Do I make you nervous for some reason?'' he inquired with an attempt at innocence. ''Are you trying to take charge of this situation?''

''Why on earth would I want to do that? This is your balloon. You're the pilot, so obviously you're in charge.'' The denial sounded incredibly weak even to her ears.

There was a disturbing gleam in his eyes. ''I wasn't referring to ballooning. I was thinking more in terms of our personal relationship.''

''We don't have a personal relationship,'' she insisted stubbornly.

''Yet.''

''Ever.''

That irksome smile was back. ''We'll see,'' he taunted.

Four

Blake's expression was so smug it set Audrey's teeth on edge. She knew that look. It was the look of a man who always, no matter what, got what he wanted.

Not this time, she vowed. He had pushed her too far. She was going to steel herself against his smooth-as-silk moves and sweet-talking words. She might have a little more trouble remaining immune to his overpowering sexiness, but she could do it if she just reminded herself that he was a no-good scoundrel. If she had a piece of paper in her purse, she'd write it a hundred, convincing times: *Blake Marshall is an unscrupulous, untrustworthy rat.*

Just when she was getting wound up, the rat spoke, his tone conciliatory. "How about a truce?"

She glared at him, but he kept right on talking in that low, pleasant, insistently seductive voice of his. "Here we are on a beautiful day, a breeze against our faces, all this gorgeous scenery and you're grumbling about kidnapping. Why not just settle back, have a glass of champagne, get to know each other better and enjoy the ride?"

"I wouldn't give you the satisfaction," she muttered obstinately, her arms folded protectively around her middle.

"Well, I hope you won't mind if I make the best of things," he said easily. Ignoring her completely, he pulled a bottle of champagne out of the cooler, popped the cork, poured himself a glass and enjoyed the view. He seemed utterly content.

Audrey gritted her teeth and scowled at his profile. She thought she caught his lips twitching with amusement. She wasn't sure what infuriated her more, his obvious determination to enjoy their situation despite her mood or the fact that he hadn't tried a little harder to persuade

her to join him. He might at least have poured
her a glass of champagne. She would have refused it, of course, maybe even thrown it back
in his smirking face, but a real gentleman would
have offered.

That was one of the problems, though. Blake
wasn't a real gentleman. She'd heard enough
about his romantic escapades, and his actions
this morning had only confirmed it. As a child
he'd probably had a streak of mischief in him
that kept his parents hopping. As a man that trait
had made him as bold and daring as any pirate.
Perversely, it was a significant part of her at-
traction toward him. If he'd been bland and polite and uninteresting, she wouldn't be torn by
these conflicting feelings. She would never have
felt this wild, urgent desire to step willingly into
his arms, a desire that warred with her common
sense and a healthy, if somewhat belated, instinct for self-preservation.

She'd just discovered that for the past year or
more she'd been deluding herself that she could
be satisfied with safe, pleasant companionship.
Now Blake had turned up with his potent masculinity, his take-charge attitude and his devilish
smile, and she recognized the absurdity of the
delusion. Those other men seemed impossibly

tame. Not one of them had made her blood roar through her veins, not one of them had made her feel dangerously, wickedly alive.

Damn the man! She'd been content with her life until this morning, pleased with the progress she'd been making to change.

She began to pace around the gondola, which caused it to sway just enough to remind her that she wasn't stalking around the man's living room in a huff. If she was going to engage in a fight at two thousand feet, there were certain concessions she was going to have to make, such as standing still.

She clung to the edge of the gondola and gazed out at the scenery—the river winding below like a tossed-aside strand of iridescent ribbon, the meadows dotted with pink and yellow and red wildflowers, the houses that looked no bigger than a child's toys. Their altitude registered in her head and was recalculated in terms of height off the ground and the potential for broken bones. She gulped and swiveled around to stare down at the floor. When he spoke she was counting slowly in an effort to calm her rapid breathing.

"I'm sorry."

The quiet words nudged their way past her

annoyance and caught her by surprise. She turned toward Blake and found that he had that sincere expression in his eyes again. It was a look that had probably gotten him out of any number of jams. She'd read someplace that he'd gone to Catholic schools as a boy. That angelic, innocent air had probably been very effective on the nuns. Goodness knows, she'd thought she'd steeled herself against it but it was still playing havoc with her heartbeat.

"What was that?" she said coolly.

"I said I was sorry."

"For what?" She had a whole list of his transgressions that required an apology. She was curious about where he'd choose to start.

"Deceiving you."

He'd picked a good one. She waited for more.

"I really did just want you along for the ride, but I should have given you a choice in the matter," he admitted contritely. He reached out a hand as if to caress her cheek, then dropped it uncertainly to his side. "I could have asked you before we ever left the ground."

A soft sigh whispered past her lips and, predictably, she detected the slightest weakening in her resistance. "Thank you for that."

"Want to explain why it made you so angry?"

She was still struggling with all the ramifications of her anger herself. She wasn't sure she wanted to get into some of them with him. "Wasn't it enough that you just carted me off without asking?"

"I'm asking you. Is that all it was?"

Blake had to force himself to stand very still while he waited for her answer. Two minutes ago he'd been tempted to sweep her into his arms and kiss her until she stopped muttering all that utter nonsense about kidnapping. He knew she would respond, more fervently than she had earlier, but something told him that using her passion as a weapon was the wrong thing to do. She was scared about more than being up here in this balloon. For some reason, she seemed to be frightened of him and her feelings for him as well.

As a boy, he'd loved animals and he'd had to learn to be patient with some of them, especially those that were wild and injured. He'd held the quivering, terrified creatures in his hands until they accepted his gentle touch, even welcomed it. He'd grown more impatient with age, more rushed, but he drew now on those early lessons in restraint.

He watched Audrey squirm uncomfortably for several minutes and when she still hadn't answered, he suggested, "Maybe we should change the subject."

She regarded him warily, but some of the tension seemed to drain from her and he knew then for certain that backing off was the right thing to do. She needed some space and he'd do his best to give it to her. The only thing he wouldn't do was walk away from her. Audrey Nelson fascinated him in some way he didn't totally understand. He wanted to know everything about her.

"Why don't you tell me how you wound up with the company?"

Relief replaced caution in her eyes. "I was looking for a change and I heard about the opening in your PR department. It seemed like the perfect answer."

The response piqued his interest. "A change from what?"

So many things, Audrey wanted to say. The past, my life. I wanted to be a new person. All she said was, "My job. It's a pretty typical story. I'd been working in a very boring position with an insurance company for several years and I hated it. There was no challenge, no fun. When...when some things happened, I decided to make a clean break of it and start over in something else.''

Surely Blake of all people would understand the need for new challenges, the need to take risks after a lifetime of caution and constant consideration for the needs of others.

''These things that happened, were they related to your job?''

With a sense of dismay, she read the concern in Blake's eyes and interpreted it as the wariness of a boss unexpectedly discovering a flaw in a trusted employee's character. That look insulted her. More than that, it hurt. ''If you're asking if I was fired, the answer is no. I was a model employee. They were sorry to see me go,'' she said stiffly.

Blake seemed surprised by her tone. ''I didn't mean that at all. I was just trying to find out why you felt the need to make such a drastic change.''

''I told you, I was bored.''

Audrey should have known it wasn't going to end at that. She'd given him an opening now and, like a dog worrying a bone, Blake was going to poke and prod into her past until he knew everything there was to know about her. Obviously he'd never read any of those etiquette columns about the rudeness of asking personal questions, although she'd never learned how to heed the columnists' advice and avoid responding.

"Wasn't there any room for advancement?" he persisted.

She sighed. "I'm sure, if I'd stayed, I would eventually have done very well."

His puzzled gaze skimmed across her face, then his eyes locked with hers. "I'm missing something."

"What could you possibly be missing? A lot of people quit their jobs and go looking for something more exciting, more rewarding. That's what I did. Harvey gave me a chance to try something I'd always wanted to do. No intrigue. Just a simple matter of moving on with my life."

Audrey mentally cursed herself the minute the words were out of her mouth. She'd practically provoked him into probing more deeply.

"Interesting choice of words," he said, exactly as she had feared her would. The man read subtleties more clearly than some people read the boldest headlines. "Did you literally make a move?"

"Yes," she said tightly. With each new piece of information, he was getting closer to the whole story. It was not an ugly one or even a particularly unusual one, but it was not a time in her life of which she was particularly proud. She settled for giving Blake the bare minimum of information, the facts, but not the emotions behind them. He'd find the basics on her personnel record anyway. "I'd been living in Seattle."

"But you wanted to get away from there, too?"

"The job was in California."

"I'm sure there are a lot of jobs in Seattle. Didn't you like it there?"

She glared at him. "Why do I have the feeling that we've gone beyond a casual get-acquainted conversation? Are you after something in particular?"

He seemed startled by her outburst. "I just want to know you better. Since you don't seem especially forthcoming with information, I'm just asking what I want to know. We can trade roles, if you like. You ask the questions for a while."

She knew she'd been reacting defensively, but Blake backed down so easily, it threw her off balance. The only questions that came to mind were far too revealing. She couldn't very well plunge right in and ask the sort of thing she really wanted to know...if he'd ever been seriously involved with anyone or something equally provocative such as whether he slept in the nude. Who knew how he'd interpret those queries and what he'd feel free to ask in turn. She settled for the obvious.

"Why did you buy the vineyard? From what I've read it was failing. You were taking an incredible risk."

He grinned. "That's exactly why I bought it. It was a challenge in something with which I'd always been fascinated. It was also in my price range. I didn't have a lot of ready cash or a lot of experience. Banks weren't going to give me a huge loan for what could be a disaster and I didn't want to take on a partner. The company and I seemed made for each other."

"You must feel very proud of the way it's turned out."

"I do, but now that Marshall wines are counted among the best in California I'm looking for new challenges," he said. His gaze lingered on her face, then drifted lower. The look practically singed her with its suggestiveness and left her breathless. She shook her head.

"You're looking in the wrong place," she finally managed to whisper raggedly.

"I don't think so. I want to get past those barriers you've put around yourself. I think there's a very special woman inside."

Blake's words warmed her, even as they terrified her. He'd made his intentions very clear and there was no place for her to run, at least not right now. If she was going to run, it would have to be very, very soon, because if Blake got any closer, if he sought more intimacy, discovered more secrets and still cared, she wasn't going to be able to resist. He was going to possess her in every nuance of the word.

"Please, Blake, let it go. You don't know me at all."

"You're right. I don't know nearly enough about you. But there's something between us and I can't just pretend it doesn't exist."

"You have to."

"Why? Why is it so clear-cut for you?"

Audrey met his gaze evenly, but if she'd hoped to stare him down, she failed miserably. "Because I knew someone exactly like you once and he was all wrong for me," she finally murmured reluctantly. "I swore I'd never make a mistake like that again."

"Someone you loved?" Blake could barely get the words past lips gone suddenly dry.

"I thought I did." She shrugged as though it hadn't mattered, but to Blake it was obvious that it had. She couldn't hide that lost, sad expression in her eyes. It touched his heart and made him angry that someone had hurt her so deeply.

"Apparently I didn't know the meaning of the word," she added with a note of wistfulness.

"What makes you think that?"

"Everything I thought I loved in him turned out to be exactly the opposite of what I needed in my life. And I certainly wasn't what he needed."

Blake watched her with a perplexed frown. "I don't understand."

"Just like you, he was strong and self-confident, a real decision maker. He seemed to have all the answers. If he wanted something, he went after it. He took risks, business and personal risks. I don't think I ever once saw him hesitate. I was attracted to those qualities, because they're all the things that I find lacking in myself."

Astonishment swept through him. "That's how you see yourself?"

"Don't you? I mean, what else could you think? I carried on about not going with you today and here I am. Doesn't that tell you anything about the courage of my convictions? I've never taken a risk in my life."

"What about leaving your home and starting over in California?"

"That wasn't so much. It was just something I had to do."

Blake shook his head impatiently. "Then let me tell you what I see. I see a woman who had the guts to tell off the president of the company she works for when she thought he was in the wrong. I see a woman who overcame her fear of ballooning and stuck with me. That's two mighty big risks in just the past couple of hours."

She waved the praise aside with a dismissive gesture. "I gave in, though. That's the bottom line. When I refused to go, I should have stuck to it. I should have been more assertive."

"Lady, if you'd been any more assertive, I'd have been out of this balloon headfirst. You were assertive enough. I just didn't want to take no for an answer." He noticed that his comment brought one of those wonderful smiles to her lips, but it faded almost instantly and it never quite reached her eyes. There were still shadows of uncertainty lurking in the violet depths.

This time he almost gave in when temptation called. He stepped toward her, wanting to soothe her, to make her his. His arms were desperate to hold her and a white-hot heat spread through him. Then, abruptly and regretfully, he reminded himself of the need for caution, and stopped. It took every bit of his strength.

"I would like very much to kiss you, Audrey Nelson," he said softly. His gaze measured her reaction, searched her eyes for the unspoken truth he knew she couldn't hide.

"But I won't if you don't want me to," he promised. "Your choice."

He stood and waited, his heart thundering in his chest, his pulse racing, and wondered what the hell he'd do, if she said no.

Five

The word *no* formed on her lips, but Audrey couldn't quite get it out.

"You don't seem to be concentrating very hard on the race," she said instead. "Didn't I just see Larry Hammond's balloon go past overhead?"

"I didn't notice," he murmured, looking right straight into her eyes.

She swallowed nervously. Well, of course, he didn't. He very definitely had other things on his mind. For example, in addition to that disconcerting, unrelenting gaze that was turning her

blood into molten honey, he was moving determinedly and provocatively toward her. Her
breath caught in her throat and she began to understand what animals felt like when they were
being stalked by deadly hunters. The urge to run
swept over her again, followed by the panicky
realization that there was no place to go.

She held out a resisting hand, but he slipped
past it and drew her tightly against him, sighing
at the contact. Their thighs were pressed together, his fingers a barely proper hairbreadth
below her breast. Her pulse took off like a well-
trained thoroughbred heading into the home-
stretch.

Blake might still be giving her a choice, but
he clearly had no intention of making it easy for
her to keep either physical or emotional distance
between them.

I ought to be flattered, she thought. The man
could have any woman he wanted and, for the
moment anyway, he seemed to want her. But
instead of feeling good that a man with Blake's
limitless choices saw something special in her,
she felt...overwhelmed. Again. It made her nervous.

If her own breathless reaction to their close-
ness was any indication, it was no wonder the

race hadn't crossed his mind in quite a while. He hadn't even glanced away when she'd mentioned it. With that smoldering blue-eyed gaze of his fixed on her, she'd barely caught sight of the competing balloon. She'd discovered that looking up was far less terrifying than looking down and much less dangerous than meeting Blake's heated glances. Once Blake did notice it, though, he was probably going to be very upset. It was her duty, she decided, to get his attention away from her and back where it belonged.

She tried to wriggle loose.

"Where are you going?" he murmured, his embrace enfolding her more tightly.

"I don't want to distract you."

"You'll distract me no matter where you are."

Under almost any other circumstances that might have been nice to hear. Up here at two thousand feet above solid ground with a man who made her head spin, it was simply heart-stopping. She didn't want him distracted, not by her, not by anything. She wanted him to guide this blasted balloon wherever it was he wanted it to go, put it down and then take her out for a very large drink. She thought she deserved it for not killing him when she'd learned the truth about this trumped-up case of mistaken identity.

To be perfectly truthful, she also didn't want him kissing her. Or maybe she wanted it too much. She thought about it and sighed. The real problem was that she'd discovered she *wanted* to feel those gentle, persuasive lips of his on hers again. Anything that tempting couldn't possibly be good for her. It was bad enough that she was addicted to chocolate.

"Why don't you want me to kiss you?" he said, as if he'd been reading her mind, instead of listening to the perfectly logical things she'd been saying aloud. She gulped.

"Who says I don't want you to kiss me?"

"You haven't said yes."

There was definitely a trap here. No wonder the man was probably going to be a multimillionaire in no time flat. He had the sharp instincts of a predator.

"Exactly," she said. "But I haven't said no either."

"Can't make up your mind?" There was a teasing glint in his eyes that irritated the dickens out of her. That challenging question infuriated her, just as he'd known it would.

"Of course, I can make up my mind," she snapped.

"Well? Yes or no." He was standing perfectly still, his body heat firing the blood in her veins, encouraging a favorable response.

Audrey took the dare. She drew in a ragged breath and murmured, "Yes."

Before he could take advantage of her reluctant agreement, she wrenched herself free of his embrace. She smiled boldly up into startled eyes. "Later."

Blake groaned in frustration and muttered something about women who wanted to have their cake and eat it, too. Audrey was rather proud of her quick thinking, but a tiny part of her was labeling her a coward. It was probably nicer than any of the names Blake was calling her under his breath.

With his back straight and shoulders tense, he retreated to the controls of the balloon. He surveyed their situation compared to the competition, then made several adjustments, pointedly ignoring her. The flames roared to life and the balloon shot up again.

Audrey knew she ought to be grateful that his attention seemed momentarily diverted by the race, but with the contrariness of a two-year-old,

she began to feel neglected. Sitting here, surrounded by stony silence, gave her too much
time to think—about herself, and about Blake.
If she'd been on the ground, she could have gone
for a nice long walk, maybe played a hard set
of tennis. Even a game of solitaire would have
been better than this thickening tension and this
ridiculous, unwarranted feeling of nagging guilt.

Worse, now that Blake was tight-lipped and
apparently determined to stay that way, she was
already beginning to miss their sparring
matches. She realized she had started enjoying
his pursuit, the mild flirting that suggested more
serious advances were in the offing.

For more than a year now, she'd been immune
to romance and essentially numb to life. Derek's
abrupt departure, amid cruel taunts about her
flaws, had left her with emotional scars, deep
wounds that had made her question the type of
woman she was. She was still asking those questions and, while she'd seen signs of improve-
ment—up until yesterday, anyway—she still
wasn't very happy with the answers.

It was something of an irony that all of the
generosity and understanding she had bestowed
on Derek had been the very things he had turned
against her. When he wanted space, she'd com-

plied. When he needed support, she had been there for him. When he strayed, she'd listened to his explanations, fought for understanding and forgiven him. She'd anticipated the man's every need, welcomed his demands because they'd given her a sense of direction. She'd felt genuine joy in the giving.

In the end, he'd hated her for it. When he left, he'd told her he wanted someone with more gumption, more self-respect. She'd thought she'd been giving him love. He had twisted it into weakness. She'd hardened her heart and sworn it would never happen again.

A gentle caress of her cheek suddenly brought her back to the present. "Hey, sweetheart, where did you go?" Blake asked, concern shadowing his eyes to a darker, even more alluring shade of blue. His anger seemed to have dissipated while her thoughts whirled back in time.

"Just a little time travel," Audrey said.

"Past or future?"

"Past."

"That's never good. Stick with the future. That's where all the promise is."

"Nice philosophy, but haven't you heard that if you ignore the past, you're destined to make the same mistakes over and over again?"

"And what mistakes have you made that were so terrible that the prospect of repeating them makes you so glum?"

"What is this? True confessions?" She tried for a light tone and a brilliant smile, but her effort didn't banish his serious expression.

"I'm no priest, but I told you before, I am a good listener. No judgments. No advice, unless you ask for it. And I give bargain basement rates."

"Isn't there an old saying about getting what you pay for?"

This time he returned her grin with a wicked gleam in his eye. "In that case, we could negotiate terms."

"Hmmm." Audrey pursed her lips thoughtfully. "I didn't bring along a lot of cash. Do you take credit cards?"

"Oh, I think we could work out better terms than that, say a kiss an hour." At her immediate frown, he added, "To be collected at the end of treatment, of course, and only if you're satisfied with the service."

Audrey sighed. The easy bantering was drawing her in again, reawakening senses that had been hibernating far too long. Blake's fingers had lingered on her cheek and his thumb brushed across her lips. The callused roughness set off a sharp tingling that was both exciting and oddly comforting. It was surprisingly good to feel alive again. She'd begun to dread the feeling, even as she'd wondered if it would ever happen again. She'd prayed her heart would never tumble crazily in her chest, that she would never experience the breathless anticipation or the heart-wrenching lows of an emotional roller-coaster ride.

Then she'd prayed she would.

Her eyes met his, caught and lingered as heat rose in her. She felt alive all right. Dangerously alive.

She blinked and asked in a husky whisper, "How are we doing in the race?"

His thumb brushed across her lips, silencing her. "Forget the race and don't try to change the subject. I want to get to know you. I can't if you keep cutting me off every time I start to get close."

"Why does it matter?" She tried to maintain an air of disinterest, but it was rougher going than she'd imagined. "After today, you'll go back to being a jet-setting playboy and I'll go back to writing copy and dreaming up PR gimmicks. Maybe we'll bump into each other in the halls.''

He winked at her. ''That raises some interesting possibilities.''

She shook her head. ''Forget it, Blake. We lead very different life-styles. Nothing's changed.''

''I don't think so. After today, I think everything will be different,'' he said with surprising gentleness. He smiled tenderly. ''For both of us.''

Audrey captured the words in her heart and held them there. Even as she clung to the warm feelings they aroused, she shook her head adamantly. ''That can't be.''

''Why not?''

''I've already explained. I'm not the sort of woman for you.''

''I think you're exactly the sort of woman for me. You don't play games. You're honest and witty and intelligent. Do you have any idea how rare that is?''

How she wished that were true. Even if it was, there were other, less attractive traits he seemed to be ignoring. It was time he faced up to them. ''I'm a wimp, remember? You'll walk all over me,'' she blurted miserably.

He stared at her in astonishment. "Why on earth would I want to do that?"

"It's not a case of your wanting to, it's just what happens when a strong person and a weak one get together. Can't you see that?"

"No, dammit." He looked as though he wanted to shake her. "I can't see it and I don't understand where you got such a crazy idea about being weak. Who put it into your head? That man you were talking about before? He must have been a real louse."

"He was right."

"I don't believe it," he said impatiently. "I haven't seen one shred of evidence to support it. Convince me."

To her utter fury, Audrey felt tears brimming in her eyes. She didn't want to play this game with him anymore. She'd opened up to Blake, shared all of her worst traits with him. If he refused to see the truth then that was his problem. It certainly wasn't his place to try to convince her that she was someone she wasn't. If she'd wanted a therapist, she would have hired one. She sure as hell didn't want one who came with strings attached and who ought to be flying this damn balloon instead of kneeling down beside her, while she moped like some ninny.

"Just go and concentrate on winning the race," she said. "Leave me alone."

He didn't budge. "I will not leave you alone. This is important. If we don't get past this image hang-up of yours, we don't stand a chance."

"If this balloon crashes, we don't stand a chance either," she pointed out. "You can do more about keeping us aloft than you can about my problems."

"We won't know that until you tell me exactly what those problems are."

"Dammit, I don't want to talk about it." She spit out each word emphatically. "Am I making myself clear?"

"Very," he said slowly, standing up. "Maybe I was wrong. Maybe you are a wimp after all."

The words fell on her with the sharpness of a well-aimed dagger. Like something that happened when you least expected it, the unfairness of Blake's comment incensed her. Instinctively, she reached out, grabbed a handful of denim and yanked him back down. She caught him off balance and he landed beside her in an awkward heap, his legs sprawled across hers in intimate abandon. She was so furious, she hardly noticed.

"I am not!" she shouted directly into his ear. With any luck it would make him go deaf. He deserved it after a crack like that. "How dare you say that? You don't even know me."

To her astonishment, instead of cowering beneath her fury the way he was supposed to, the irritating man was chuckling, his face split with a wide grin. He definitely looked like an Irish rogue on a winning streak.

"Apparently I know you better than you know yourself," he said with annoying smugness.

"Are you trying to make a point?" she growled at him suspiciously.

"I just did."

"Exactly what do you think you've proved?"

"You are a very unlikely wimp, Audrey Nelson. With that sharp tongue of yours you could strike terror into entire armies. Now, that's the last I want to hear about it." His implacable expression indicated he wouldn't tolerate any argument on the subject. Audrey glowered back at him, until at last he grinned at her.

"Armies, huh?" she said.

"At the very least. Now stand up here with me," he urged, getting to his feet with a quick, lithe movement. "Take a look around. Let's stop all the heavy philosophical stuff and just concentrate on enjoying the day. When was the last time you simply relaxed and enjoyed yourself? Harvey probably hasn't given you a vacation in years.''

"He gave me one," she muttered dryly. "I'm supposed to be on it now."

"What happened?"

She shook her head. "It doesn't matter. I'm going to take a few days here, after the race."

"Let's start that vacation now." He held out his hand. After an instant's hesitation, she put her hand in his and allowed herself to be drawn up. They stood in silence. Toe to toe. Hand in hand. The air grew thick with a sweet, unbearable tension. With his free hand, Blake reached out a tentative finger to brush a stray lock of dark hair out of her eyes. That finger was warm and trembling as it skimmed her cheek.

"I know I promised it was going to be your choice, but I'm not sure I can keep from kissing you," he said with such gentleness and longing that Audrey's heart stilled.

Despite fear, despite anger, despite everything, she wanted that kiss as much as he did. More, perhaps, because it had been so long since she'd felt this yearning, this dull, sweetly tormenting ache deep inside. Eyes locked with his, she lifted his hand to her lips and brushed a kiss across his knuckles. The gesture, meant as an answer, set off a trembling in him and a harsh moan rumbled deep in his throat.

"You're sure I'm not pressuring you?"

Audrey gave him a shaky grin. "Hey, don't let that stop you now."

"I will stop, if it's what you want."

"No, please. It's okay. I don't understand it and I'm not sure I like it, but I know exactly what I want. I want you to kiss me." She hesitated. "Very much."

With a deep sigh of satisfaction, Blake closed his eyes and drew her close. The urgency abated. He wanted to savor every moment she was in his arms, even if she was filled with uncertainty. He wanted to delight in her fresh, clean scent that hinted of spring flowers, in the clarity of those vivid violet eyes, the feel of her warm, gently curved body pressed against the throbbing, demanding heat of his own flesh.

Lord, she felt so good held close like this, it was as though she belonged. The rightness astounded him, sent his senses reeling. He'd felt these same sharp stirrings of excitement before, but never the tenderness, the protectiveness that had almost immediately surfaced with Audrey. He knew the protectiveness was something he would have to deal with later, that Audrey was a woman who wouldn't welcome him in the role of guardian. She had things to prove to herself and he had no right to stand in her way. It was the only way she would rid herself of those foolish insecurities.

For now, though, he found the combination of feelings swirling through him irresistible. This second, more volatile kiss was inevitable.

He searched her face for any sign of lingering hesitation or regret and, finding none, he breathed a soft sigh of relief. Able to wait no longer for the taste of her, he pressed his lips to her forehead, to the tiny furrows in her brow that came, he suspected, from fretting far too much about inconsequential things. With the touch of his lips, he hoped to ease the worrying. The silkiness of her skin lured him on, next to her cheeks, then to the tip of her nose and, when her eyelids had fluttered closed, to each of those in turn.

By the time he reached the generous curve of her mouth, her own lips had parted for him and what began in gentleness escalated quickly into fire and hunger. Mere acceptance of his touch became ardent demand. Her teeth were sharp and teasing against his invading tongue and he felt her body tremble from head to toe. His flesh burned with the heat of her touch and his muscles tightened in anticipation of all that was to come. With that potent kiss, they shared breath and need and life.

"Blake! Dammit, Blake, what the devil are you up to now?"

John's irritated, anxious words on the radio slashed across the moment's tenderness, cooled passion more effectively than an icy shower.

"Damn!" Blake muttered, as he grabbed the radio. He kept one arm firmly around Audrey's waist, his hand splayed on the curve of her hip. To his relief, she didn't draw away immediately. In fact, her gaze traveled over his face at leisure, her eyes wide, as though she'd been as startled as he was by the intensity of the kiss.

"Blake!"

"John, you've got a lousy sense of timing."

"If my timing were any worse, you'd be getting your feet wet in another few minutes."

His eyes still locked with Audrey's, Blake inquired distractedly and without much interest, "What are you talking about?"

"You're losing altitude. I thought at first you were heading down to a better current, but you've been dropping for too long now. I don't like the looks of it. Is there some sort of problem?''

That brought him out of his trance. Blake glanced out and saw that they were, indeed, lower than any of the other balloons in the vicinity. He couldn't even spot the blue and gold of Larry Hammond's entry.

''Where's Hammond?''

''Forget Hammond for the moment, unless you want to take a dunking in the creek.''

That woke Audrey up. The dazed expression in her eyes faded. ''What creek?'' she said, suddenly trying to free herself to get a look. Blake knew she wasn't going to like what she saw one bit. He wasn't exactly thrilled about it himself. He tried to nestle her head in the curve of his shoulder, but she was having none of it.

''I want to see!'' She peered past him and her body sagged in his arms, as she murmured, ''Oh, dear heaven, we're going down in a river. We are going to drown.'' She glared at him and repeatedly punched a finger square in the middle of his chest. ''And if we do, Blake Marshall, I'm going to give you a very nasty time of it.''

He tried not to chuckle at the threat, because she was obviously so serious about it. ''It's a piddly little creek,'' he observed pointedly.

"Even if we were to go down in it—which we're not going to—there's no way you're going to drown."

Black brows arched in feminine skepticism. "You don't mind if I ask John about that, do you?"

"Don't you trust me?"

"Your track record for the day isn't exactly top of the line."

"When have I lied to you?"

"Let me count the times," she muttered darkly. "Would you just stop bickering with me and get this thing headed in the right direction."

"It wasn't so long ago that you thought down was the right direction."

"That was before we had a raging river underneath us."

"It is not..."

The radio crackled. "Blake, have you found the problem yet?"

Blake knew perfectly well what the problem was. It didn't take a genius to figure it out. He'd been so infatuated with Audrey, so lost in the sensuality of that kiss that he'd let the air—in the balloon, anyway—cool too long. All he needed to do was send another long burst of hot air into the envelope and they'd be flying high again. He might have been foolish, but they were certainly in no real danger, despite Audrey's conviction that they were about to be well past their earlobes in swirling, violent white-water rapids.

"No problem," he told John, casting a significant glance at Audrey as he spoke. He urged her toward the side, then went to turn on the propane tank.

That was when he noticed the problem. "Oh, hell," he muttered before he could catch himself.

Audrey was leaning over his shoulder before he could take his next breath. "What?"

"Nothing."

"'*Oh, hell*' is not nothing. It is most definitely something. I want to know what."

This was no time to start getting distracted, but he tried to give her hand a reassuring squeeze. She shook it off. "Blake! You can't placate me like some child. If we're going down, I deserve to know the truth. I might have plans to make or something."

He just barely managed to restrain a chuckle. His lips twitched, though, and she caught it. She frowned.

"Sorry," he said. "I'm not trying to placate

Six

"**W**hat do you mean the pilot light went out?" Audrey asked. She was particularly proud that no note of hysteria had crept into her voice. She was saving it for later—when they crashed in the river.

After all, Blake had looked perfectly calm when he made the announcement. Then again, it was obvious he was in a big hurry to get the thing lit and it wasn't because he had a turkey ready for the oven. This pilot light of his apparently did something important. On second thought, perhaps she ought to be screaming her head off.

"Blake, you're not answering me again. Explain about this pilot light."

"I mean the damn thing went out," he muttered, fiddling intently with something she couldn't quite see and wasn't sure she wanted to.

"Let me try that question another way: does it matter?"

He glanced up at her. "You're not going to like the answer to that."

"Oh, dear heaven," she murmured.

"Don't go getting crazy on me. I haven't had one of these crash on me yet."

Suddenly Audrey noticed that puffy white clouds, which had been drifting pleasantly overhead, seemed to be receding at a rather alarming rate. "Then why are we falling?" she managed in a choked whisper, trying to decide if it was auspicious that her entire life was not flashing before her eyes yet.

"Because the air is cooling off."

The significance of that did not slip past her. Hot air rises, cool air...dear God! "I don't suppose you'd like to borrow some matches?"

Blake shot her a quick, encouraging grin. "Hang on to that sense of humor, sweetheart."

"Is there anything else I should hang on to?"

"You could try me," he suggested hopefully. The look he cast in her direction was so steamy it could have heated an entire room. Unfortunately, it didn't seem to help the air in the balloon, though it certainly warmed her from her head to her toes. She could feel her cheeks flush. She ran the tip of her tongue over dry lips.

"And break your concentration?" she said with sheer bravado. "Not a chance. Unless I miss my guess, that's exactly what got us into this mess."

She leaned out of the gondola to decide whether it was time to start praying—or jump. The tops of what she hoped were some very tall trees appeared to be no more than the length of a football field below them. She could hear what was very definitely the roar of the raging river, though on closer inspection she had to admit it did appear to be somewhat smaller and more shallow than she'd first thought. That observation required only a minor adjustment in her dire imaginings. She'd probably die plummeting headfirst onto the jagged rocks, instead of drowning. She was glad she'd had that last sizzling kiss before she went.

Then she decided it was better not to look and clamped her hands over her eyes. She could feel the balloon dropping at a speed no doubt faster than any ton of lead. Images of imminent contact with treetops and swirling water flashed through her mind with sickening clarity. Just when she was convinced there was no hope for them, she heard the sputter, then the roar of a timely spurt of flame. The balloon seemed to catch the air like an opening parachute and the downward plummeting slowed.

So, finally, did her heartbeat, as they began to climb again.

She parted the fingers she was holding over her eyes and peeked at Blake. "Is that going to happen again?"

"I hope not."

"I don't suppose you could inject a little more certainty into your voice?"

"It's a common enough occurrence. Every pilot knows how to deal with it." He gestured toward the ground, which was dropping away again. "See, we're not in any danger. We're on our way back up. No problem."

"Unless you count the fact that my heart

stopped beating for a few minutes, then made up for it by slamming against my ribs like a freight train. That can't possibly be healthy.''

He surveyed her with disconcerting thoroughness, starting with her mouth, drifting lower to linger on her breasts, then on, right straight down to her toes. ''Everything working okay now?''

Everything was tingling, but she wasn't about to tell him that. ''I'm not sure.'' To her disgust, her voice came out all quivery.

''Come here and let me check.''

She groaned at the seductive gleam in his eyes. ''Don't you ever think about anything else?''

Blake seemed to consider the question carefully. ''Nope. Not since you turned up this morning. Before that, though, my mind was entirely on this race.''

''You know you have a fascinating array of seduction techniques, Mr. Marshall. Perhaps we should try marketing those to one of the men's magazines...*101 Ways to Get a Woman into Your Arms.* How do you think Harvey would feel about that?''

''Forget Harvey. I'd hate it. Besides, I'd rather think of some way to keep her there. My technique at that must need work. You keep running away from me.''

"It should give you no end of satisfaction to know that as long as we're up here, I won't get far.''

"Eventually, we'll have to land,'' he said, his expression suddenly sobering. Her pulse fluttered, as his voice softened and strummed lightly over her nerves. "What happens then, Audrey? Will you run?''

She should. Every instinct told her that it would be the smart thing to do, but, Lord, she didn't want to. Blake was making her feel special again. He was making her feel like a woman. Flames, even brighter and more dangerous than before, spiraled through her at the mere thought of his touches.

"Hot,'' she murmured abruptly, tugging her sweatshirt over her head to reveal a scoop-necked sleeveless T-shirt. She caught the blazing look in Blake's eyes and grabbed a plastic plate from inside the cooler and began fanning herself. Blake might have concluded she wasn't a wimp by now, but he was going to think she was nuts. Would he still want her then?

"I'd be glad to help you cool off,'' he offered, lifting the top of the cooler as he sat down next to her. So far, he seemed to be taking her actions in stride. Apparently he was a very tolerant man.

"How?"

"Just lean back and close your eyes."

"Shouldn't you be making sure we get back on course for the race?"

"I've done that. Now hush." He pressed a finger to her lips and she obediently closed them. "Shut your eyes."

At the hypnotic purr of his voice her eyes drifted closed, then snapped open. One dark brow lifted warily. "I'm not sure I can trust a man who doesn't want me to see what he's up to."

"If you're hot, what I have in mind is better than air-conditioning."

Audrey wasn't sure her overheated flesh had anything to do with the temperature, but she was willing to give him a chance to lower her body's thermostat—as long as he didn't touch her. One fleeting caress and she'd be done for. She'd melt into a little puddle and that was all they'd find of her when the balloon landed. Blake would have a lot of explaining to do over that.

It might be worth it, she decided with a sigh and obligingly closed her eyes.

Suddenly a trickle of icy water slid along the

curve of her shoulder, crept past her collarbone, then ran in a cooling rivulet between her breasts. Her eyes snapped open, accompanied by a startled gasp. Blake was sitting next to her, his face flushed, his concentration intense as he held an ice cube over her. The look of absolute fascination on his face was enough to make her pulse skitter crazily.

"Just sit still," he urged gently as he trailed the cube very, very slowly along the sensitive flesh on the inside of her arm. Her skin cooled, but an unexpectedly fiery sensation shot straight through to her abdomen.

With the lightest of touches, he marked a path along the scooped neckline of her T-shirt and Audrey felt her nipples harden to sensitive buds as they did on a chilly morning. Blake's gaze fell on the peaks that strained against the lightly ribbed fabric and his lips curved into a satisfied smile. Her eyes widened, met his and she glanced away. She was afraid he would read too much in her eyes, would know that her senses were responding all too readily.

"Feels good, doesn't it?" he asked huskily.

"Umm," she murmured noncommittally, not wanting him to stop, but afraid to allow him to go on. The exquisite sensations building in her were so sharp and intense they were impossible to resist, though, once more, she told herself that if she was to stay in control of her own fate, she had to.

When she uttered no real protest, Blake continued on relentlessly. The trail across her skin was icy cold, yet it was leaving a white-hot path of heat in its wake. Audrey's muscles tensed as her sensitized flesh waited for the next touch, the next slow stroke of fire and ice.

She felt Blake's fingers at her waist, then the quick tug as he pulled her shirt from the waistband of her pants. Her hand automatically reached out to stop him, but he stilled her gesture and lifted the shirt barely an inch, just enough to trace a delicate line across her bare belly with the ice. Tension coiled more tightly within her as she tried to anticipate where the next touch would come.

Too much, she thought. The feelings were too raw, too intense. She had to stop them before they whirled out of control, before they led her down a path she wasn't ready to travel. Much more of this and she'd drag him down on the floor of the gondola again, and this time, instead of yelling in his ear, she'd have her way with him.

Deftly, she reached her hand into the cooler and picked up her own handful of ice, quickly slipping it inside the collar of Blake's shirt, where it slid down his back and lodged at the waistband of his jeans.

His eyes widened in shock and his outraged gasp brought an immediate end to his own uneven breathing. He yanked his shirt loose so the ice fell free. Then he glowered at her, reaching for more ice of his own.

"So that's the way you want to play, Ms. Nelson." His voice was laced with laughter and feigned menace.

She scooted out of his reach. "No, honest. I didn't mean it." She covered her breasts, but couldn't figure out how to keep his approaching hands away from her back.

"You didn't mean to drop that ice down my back?" The deep-throated, disbelieving rasp of his voice sent a shiver along her spine. "I suppose you just found it in your hand and didn't know what else to do with it?"

"Something like that," she mumbled, trying to quiet the laughter that threatened to bubble up. He looked so indignant, to say nothing of disappointed. He hadn't expected his ardor to cool quite so radically.

"Uh-uh. I'm not buying it and you, my sweet, are going to pay."

"Pay?" she repeated, her voice quivering slightly. "How?"

There was a wicked gleam in his eyes as he held the ice just beyond her reach for a tormenting eternity, before finally dropping it at her feet to melt. "On second thought, I think I'll just let you wait and see."

Audrey watched the puddle form and had the strangest sensation that she'd have been better off with that ice dumped inside her T-shirt. "Blake Marshall, this is not some game."

"Isn't it?"

Maybe it was, but if so, the rules were all new to her. She thought she'd be safer playing Monopoly, but she doubted if Blake would sit still for a competition over a mythical Park Place or Boardwalk. Buying up property had become commonplace to him. He'd added hundreds of acres to the vineyard since he first purchased it. She, on the other hand, represented a challenge.

Audrey knew a few things about men and challenges. They often lost interest, once they'd gotten what they wanted. And the more you fought them, the higher you made the stakes, the more determined they became to get what they wanted. It had something to do with that ridiculous macho stubbornness.

Knowing that was all very nice, but it didn't solve her problem. There would be a huge risk in giving in to Blake. If she took away the challenge and hoped that he'd vanish once the thrill of the chase was gone, she'd probably be head over heels in love with the man before the game ended. He was already clambering over walls she'd thought were too high to be breached.

Perhaps that was the only choice she had. She could give in and then try very hard to show Blake that she wasn't the woman for him. She was no adventurer who would thrill to taking risks, and he would grow quickly bored with the simple life she'd chosen for herself. It was a risk she was going to have to consider.

But not now. Now she was going to savor what was left of their day together, accept whatever it had to offer. The memories would be something she could recall on cold winter nights when she was fighting loneliness and boredom.

"Hungry?" he asked, interrupting her thoughts. "There's some cold chicken in the cooler."

"No, thanks. This is no time for a picnic."

"Why not?"

"Because picnics are supposed to be on the ground, maybe in a park or at the beach."

"Who made up that rule?"

"It doesn't matter," she said stubbornly. "It's just one of those things that sensible people know."

"I see," he said. He nodded sagely, but she saw the tiny suggestion of a smirk on his face before he added persuasively, "I'm sure there's a park down there somewhere."

"But we're not in it. In fact, do you have any idea where we are now?"

"Oh, I'd say we're about halfway to Glenwood Springs."

"Any sign of Larry Hammond?"

"Nope." He didn't sound particularly distressed.

"I'm sorry."

"Don't be. This has turned into more fun than any race I've been in before."

"But you're going to lose."

"You can prevent that," he retorted with a look that was pure invitation.

"I meant the race."

He grinned at her. "What did you think I meant?"

She squirmed uncomfortably. "Never mind."

"It won't matter so much, if you console me."

She shot him an indignant look. "I have no intention of consoling you," she warned, then taunted deliberately, "Frankly, you deserve to lose. You haven't been paying one bit of attention to what you were supposed to be doing. Seems to me like all this media hype about what a hotshot competitor you are was pure hokum."

"Hokum?" Blake's voice rose ominously.

She ignored his tone and doubled the implied dare. "That's right. You get some woman up here with you, your libido takes over and it's goodbye race. It must not have meant as much to you as I thought. The media will have a field day when they discover that you lost not only to Larry Hammond, but to half a dozen others, just because you couldn't keep your mind on what you were doing."

Blake sputtered indignantly, but she kept right on. "Of course, it will fit right in with that image of yours as a womanizer. Just try to keep my name out of it."

"Are you trying to egg me on? Do you actually care whether I win this race?"

"Not for myself," she said blithely, leaning back staring up at the inside of the huge balloon.

She didn't dare look him in the eyes. "I just want to get back on the ground."

He grinned at her and nodded. "I see. Very clever." He paused, then asked, "Are you sure you're not just the least bit concerned about my feelings?"

"Don't go getting any ideas, Marshall. I'll admit I thought it was important to you, but obviously that's not the case." She allowed the charge to hang in the air, then prodded quietly, "What about John Harley and this Jenkins, though? Don't you owe it to them to at least try?"

"Why are you so worried about them? You don't even know Harley and Jenkins."

"That doesn't mean I don't have a sense of honor. From what I gathered, John Harley has done a lot for you. He seems to think you're pretty special. And you said Jenkins put up part of the money for your entry. Of course, if that doesn't matter to you..."

"It matters," he muttered, studying her curiously, as though not quite sure what to make of her change in attitude. "I don't know, though. It's probably too late."

"So you're a quitter, too?" She shrugged. "Of course, you won't know that it's too late until you've given it your best shot. I don't want you blaming me later for breaking your winning streak.''

His gaze roved over her thoughtfully, then he grinned and jumped to his feet. The look of the adventurer was back and something in Audrey thrilled to that look. ''Okay, lady,'' he said finally. ''Let's go for it.''

Audrey moved to his side, gazing around at the other balloons in the vicinity, and watched with a sense of awe as they fell back one by one. For the first time all day, she was truly caught up in the excitement. She hardly noticed that they'd climbed higher than ever before or that the land below was passing by at a faster and faster clip. With Blake next to her, she felt astonishingly safe.

Perhaps it was because he'd brought them through that potential crisis without a scratch. More likely it was simply because she was coming to trust him. He'd kept his word all day. he hadn't pushed her beyond what she'd been willing to accept, though she knew the restraint had cost him, just as it had cost her.

''Blake!'' John's voice crackled over the radio again. ''Where are you headed? I'm losing sight of you.''

"I'm going over the ridge to check out the currents over there. Don't worry about it. I'll maintain radio contact."

"Don't do it."

"I have to. It may be the only way I'll ever catch up to Hammond."

"Come on, man. It's not worth it. You know what the roads are like. If anything happens over there, we won't be able to get to you. We'll have to come in on foot or call out one of the helicopters."

"Nothing is going to happen," he said, draping an arm around Audrey's shoulders. "I've got my good luck charm with me." To her amazement, she accepted the reassurance as fact. John's fears didn't faze her. If anything, they only added to an astonishing sense of giddiness, an exciting edge of anticipation.

She was actually taking a daredevil's risk and enjoying it. She'd probably come unglued later when she realized what she'd done, but right now, she only wanted Blake to have his chance at winning and she was thrilled at the prospect of being by his side when it happened.

"John, give me a reading on Hammond's location," Blake said patiently. He understood the man's hesitation, but he was determined to have his way on this.

John, still muttering indignantly, gave him a rough idea of how far ahead his chief rival was. There were others ahead as well, but they didn't worry him nearly as much. Blake heaved a sigh of relief. It wasn't quite as bad as he'd feared. This shortcut should give him a chance of passing the others and catching Hammond.

In fact, the only thing between him and a victory now were the dark clouds gathering on the horizon. He figured he had less than an hour before the storm broke. If the race wasn't over by then, the rain would force him down.

Speeding along on the far side of the ridge out of sight of the others gave him an often longed-for sense of isolation. Having Audrey standing so bravely next to him brought him utter contentment.

There was so much they had to learn about each other, but for the first time he had a feeling she was going to give them the time to make such discoveries. Her unexpected shift in attitude opened up limitless possibilities for the two of them.

He gazed down at her upturned face and caught the excitement sparkling in her eyes.

"Having fun?"

"Yes," she said and he chuckled at the note of surprise in her voice.

"You're not afraid anymore?"

"No," she admitted and grinned back at him. "Astonishing, isn't it? You must have worked some magic on me."

"Maybe you're just learning to test your own limits."

She hesitated as she apparently considered what he said thoughtfully, then nodded. "Maybe so. I just hope you don't have any more tests in store for this afternoon."

Blake's gaze shifted uneasily to the horizon, where the clouds were turning blacker and more ominous. "I hope not," he murmured.

She clearly caught the caution in his voice. "*Hope?* You can't do any better than that?"

"Now, look," he began. "I don't want you to panic or anything, but I want to be honest with you."

She stiffened beside him. "I don't think I'm going to like this."

"You told me to stop treating you like a child. That's what I'm doing. I want you to be prepared."

"*Prepared?* Prepared for what?" Her voice rose and that spark of delight in her eyes faded.

A bolt of lightning split the sky ahead, followed by the distant rumble of thunder.

"Oh, dear heaven," she murmured unsteadily. She grabbed his arm and held on so tightly, he was sure he'd have little half-moon scars where her nails were digging in. "What happens now?"

"Nothing if we can outrun the storm and land." Another crash of thunder punctuated his response.

Audrey's eyes blinked wide. "I don't like the sound of that."

"It's still way off in the distance. We have plenty of time."

"I'm not talking about the thunder. I'm talking about what you said...*if* we can outrun the storm. Is there some reason we might not be able to?"

He took a deep breath and tried to ignore the pain in his arm where she was still clinging to him. "I'll be honest with you. The winds could shift before we find a suitable place to land. If it starts raining very hard, we'll have to go down wherever we are. It's risky being up here in a storm."

"How risky?"

"The wind can knock us into a power line. Then there's the lightning...."

Audrey groaned. "Never mind about the lightning. I get the idea. Is there some reason you decided to pick now to be honest with me?" she grumbled. "For once, it might have been nice to hear one of those vague, but upbeat reassurances of yours. Maybe it's time you blindfolded me. Isn't that what kidnappers are supposed to do with their victims?"

"You're no victim and you know it." The breeze was ruffling her black curls and he brushed them back from her face. "We'll be fine. Even if we have to take the balloon down sooner than I'd like, John will come after us."

"Don't try to kid me. I heard what he said. He can't bring the truck on this side of the ridge. They'll have to come in on foot. It could take days, maybe even weeks. Do you know anything about what berries we can eat?"

He grinned at her. "I doubt we'll need to hunt for berries to keep from starving. That creek down there is probably loaded with fish."

"And I suppose you brought along a fishing pole?"

His face fell. "Well, no. But we can improvise. I don't understand what all the fuss is about. Would it be so awful spending a night under the stars with me?''

"In the pouring rain?" she responded incredulously. "Do you even have to ask?"

"These storms never last. We can make a campfire. We have food and wine."

"For tonight. What about tomorrow?"

"Hush," he whispered. He ran a finger across her lips and added provocatively, "It would be very romantic."

"And cold," she reminded him. "It would also be very cold."

"We could keep each other warm."

The notion didn't seem to appease her. If anything, she looked as though she was beginning to suspect that this was some devious scheme he'd had in mind from the first.

"Audrey, don't even think it."

"Think what?"

"I did not mean for us to get stranded out here. If this is anybody's fault, it's nature's."

"We aren't stranded yet," she reminded him. "And if you're very smart, Blake Marshall, you'll see that we aren't."

That was the precise moment when a sudden gust of wind blew the first huge drops of very cold rain in their faces.

Seven

"**A**re you splashing water around again to test the air currents?" Audrey asked hopefully.

"No." Blake's tone was disturbingly curt and his tight-lipped expression was not one bit reassuring.

Her mind made a deft leap to a terrifying conclusion. "We're going to crash, aren't we?" Her voice was amazingly calm for a woman who'd just gone into panic. She was clearly tapping inner resources she'd never known she possessed.

"No." He apparently caught the disbelief in her eyes, because he tilted her face up until their gazes clashed. "I promise. We're going to land perfectly safely...as soon as I find an open field away from the power lines."

He picked up the radio. "John, are you there?"

"I've been here all day, boss. You just haven't been listening. Ain't it about time for you to bring that sucker down?"

"I was just thinking the same thing. Any ideas?"

"You're the one with the view. Where are you?"

"You mean you can't see me?"

Blake's question was greeted with an extraordinary variety of muffled curses before John finally calmed down and said, "I've been telling you that for the past hour, but you had to go and get yourself behind a mountain range. What the hell have you been doing up there?"

Audrey's heart raced anxiously and she shot him a warning look. "I hope you don't plan on answering that question."

He grinned at her. Covering the radio with his hand, he said in a low voice, "Don't worry, sweetheart. I never kiss and tell."

Audrey regarded him skeptically, but her pulse readjusted to something close to normal.

"Blake, where did you go?" John interrupted impatiently. "Answer me."

Blake winked at her. "I'm trying to come up with a plan. Give me a minute."

"How about I try to reach some of the other pilots and see if they can spot you?"

"Try it, but I don't think it'll do any good. I can't see any of the others. They must be up ahead or on the other side of the ridge. I'm just going to look for a spot to land. There's a clearing to my left that looks okay. I'll let you know after I check it out."

"How's Audrey doing?"

Blake glanced at her with something that looked like admiration in his eyes. "She's great."

"Good. You tell that pretty little thing not to worry. You two just sit tight and we'll be in after you. Once the storm lets up, we can get a copter to fly over. You have some of those flares with you?"

"Sure, but we shouldn't need them. This storm should break while there's still plenty of daylight."

"Not according to the weather bureau. There's one of them fronts passing through. This could go on all night."

"Then start the search in the morning. There's no point in taking foolish risks. We'll be fine overnight. I've got emergency supplies."

"Let's just wait and see, then."

Now that she had accepted the fact that they were actually being forced down, Audrey found that she wasn't the least bit frightened, not even by the prospect of being stranded overnight. Obviously, that was because Blake and John were treating it so matter-of-factly and, admittedly, because Blake would be with her. He might stir a restless excitement in her that bore watching, but he would never knowingly cause her any harm. She knew that as certainly as she knew that the rain was splattering down a bit harder with every second that passed.

"What can I do to help?" she asked, still basking in Blake's praise and wanting to do everything she could to deserve it.

Blake gave her one of those encouraging, heart-stopping smiles. "Not a thing. Just sit back and relax. We should be on the ground in no time."

Even though she was facing the forced landing calmly, Audrey wasn't quite prepared to sit back and relax, not with dark clouds rolling toward them and lightning splitting the sky every few seconds. She wanted to know what was going on every minute. Standing to one side of the gondola out of Blake's way, she watched as they drifted down, catching various currents that pulled them back and forth to keep them headed straight toward the center of the clearing.

"I hope I do as well as this on Sunday," Blake muttered as he maneuvered down.

"What are you talking about?"

"One part of the competition is a target hit, exactly like this, only without the rain and wind gusts. One balloonist drops a target and the rest of us have to try to come in as close to it as we can get."

"I'm so glad you have this wonderful opportunity to get in some practice," Audrey said dryly. Then her stomach rolled over as a particularly strong wind gust dragged them wildly off course and the skies opened up to dump rain down in torrents.

"Blake, are we going to land on top of those aspens?" Brushing her rain-soaked hair out of her face, she asked as though it were merely a matter of mild curiosity.

"Not if I can help it."

She nodded at his cautious phrasing, took note of their current low altitude and muttered under

her breath, "We're going to land on the trees."
She waited for the first throat-clutching sign of
hysteria, but it didn't come.

It wouldn't be too awful, she told herself with
something surprisingly akin to serenity. The aspens weren't all that high and they'd probably
just sort of dangle there like a free-hanging tree
house. It might be kind of fun. Another adventure to tell the grandchildren about…if she lived
long enough to marry and have kids. If lightning
didn't strike the trees.

Oh, dear heaven.

At the last second, with the silvery aspen
leaves not all that far from her fingertips, a draft
of air carried the gondola clear of the trees,
though the balloon tangled in the branches of
those along the edge of the field. They landed
with an unexpected, jarring thump that threw her
to her knees.

Blake was beside her in an instant, his eyes
filled with concern. Audrey had always thought
it would be interesting to live around one of
those men who blithely led a woman into danger
and then stuck around to comfort her when it
got especially rough. You either wound up with
nerves of steel or an ulcer, but at least he was
there to hold your hand.

Blake, however, was not exactly holding her hand. He was running his hands along her thighs, in what she was sure he meant to be some sort of medical examination. Unfortunately, it was having the nerve-tightning effect of seduction. She tried to slap his hands away before they both started getting ideas.

He peered at her closely. "Are you okay?"

"Nothing's broken and we're on the ground, what could possibly be wrong?" she responded with a jaunty smile. "I suppose it's too much to hope that you've figured out exactly what ground we're on."

"I know we're in Colorado."

"Very funny."

He caressed her damp cheeks. "Seriously, if you're okay, I want to call John and let him know we landed safely. Then we'll see what we can do about waiting out this storm."

While Blake was talking to John, Audrey glanced at her watch. It was just before noon. If the storm broke soon there would be plenty of daylight left for a rescue. John had to be wrong about the weather staying like this through the night. She'd heard people talking earlier at the rodeo grounds. They said summer storms came and went here, leaving the air fresh and cool, the sky an even clearer blue. The thunder and lightning and wind-whipped rain almost never lingered for hours on end.

This time it did.

Every white bolt of lightning and accompanying crash of thunder rattled Audrey's frayed nerves until she was as jumpy as a cat, beneath the tarp which Blake had used to cover them. After a while, she realized it wasn't so much the storm as it was the growing tension and electricity arcing between her and Blake in the confined space of the gondola.

Though she carefully kept their conversation on impersonal topics, every word, every phrase seemed to be rich with significance, innuendos or blatant suggestiveness. Even when they laughed together, there was something about the sound that wove the sensual web around them more tightly. She was certain that a single spark would set them ablaze.

It had something to do with the way Blake looked at her. His surveys were slow and caressing, even when his hands were not. There was heated desire in his eyes, even when his humor was its lightest, his smile its most innocent. And Audrey's flesh responded to the touches that never came, as surely as it would have to reality. At times she felt as if the electricity building inside her would crack and rumble and split the air as dramatically as the lightning.

Dusk came before they knew it, along with a break in the storm that gave them a fleeting glimpse of a breathtakingly brilliant sunset of pink and orange and golden slashes that teased the horizon, then disappeared with a final wink of palest mauve. Sitting side by side in the gondola, they watched in awe and lifted glasses of wine in a silent toast.

"Let's see if we can find a little dry wood and build a camp fire," Blake suggested, when the spectacular moment ended. "I doubt they'll come looking for us tonight, not if there are more storms in the area."

Delighted at the prospect of activity, Audrey allowed Blake to lift her out of the gondola with arms just as strong and sure as she'd imagined. He held her just a moment longer than necessary and when he set her down, her legs were ridiculously unsteady. Unwilling to face the truth, she blamed the trembling on being cramped for so long in one position. She shook her legs to stir the circulation, then followed Blake into the grove of aspen, ignoring the smug grin she thought she'd seen in his eyes.

The earth had a damp, clean scent, but it was uneven under their feet and with twilight fading rapidly, they made a quick game of finding twigs and branches that weren't too soaked, taking their haul back out to the clearing.

"Now what?" Audrey asked.

"We build a fire."

"How?"

Blake regarded her curiously. "Haven't you ever been camping?"

"Never."

"Weren't you a Girl Scout or something, when you were a kid?"

"Nope. My mother was into piano lessons and embroidery for little girls. She had some lovely samplers on the wall at home." There was a wry twist of her lips as she recalled the endless, tedious hours of cross-stitches and the inept final results.

"I thought that attitude went out in another century."

"It did, everywhere except in our household. My mother had very rigid ideas about proper behavior and practical skills. Cooking was practical, because it was the way to a man's heart.

Piano was okay, because it was a pleasant way to spend an evening. She couldn't imagine what use a woman would find for math beyond balancing a checkbook.''

"And your father?"

"He died when I was seven. It was just my mother, my sister and me."

"How did your sister turn out?"

"She found it even more incredibly oppressive than I did. She ran away when she was fourteen and joined a circus."

Blake laughed. "You're kidding."

"Nope. She became a trapeze artist, until she got married and settled down in Iowa. She had a brief rebellion, but now she's just the sort of lady my mother wanted us to be. She belongs to the PTA, bakes pies for the church bake sales and last I heard she was starting a quilting circle."

"Are you still rebelling?"

"No. Not exactly. I'm just trying to find out what I'm made of. I've spent too much of my life trying to please other people, first my mother, then…" She hesitated. "Then the man I was involved with. Everybody wants approval, but I've made a career of sublimating my own needs to get it. That relationship proved to me that I'd better find out if I have any strengths at all.''

''Learned anything today?'' Blake asked, pointedly avoiding her gaze as he arranged the twigs for a fire.

She thought about the question for a long time and Blake let the silence build until she said, ''I think maybe I have.''

''Such as?''

''I'm not quite the coward I thought I was. Not that I wasn't scared to death when I first realized we'd taken off back in Snowmass, but I survived it.''

''Good start,'' he said, then handed her some of the firewood. ''Now how about finishing this fire and getting it started.''

''I don't...'' She caught a glimpse of his challenging expression and shrugged. ''Okay, but don't yell if it's lopsided and goes out in five minutes.''

''Promise,'' he agreed solemnly.

When she'd built a respectable fire, Blake brought out the cooler, which still contained chicken and another bottle of wine.

''I'm starving,'' Audrey said, her voice edged with surprise.

"It's no wonder. You wouldn't touch anything when I offered it to you earlier."

"I was being stubborn."

"Yes, I remember," he said. "I'm glad you're more amenable now. I'd hate to be stuck out here with a grouch."

"I am never a grouch," she said haughtily.

"Oh, that's right," he corrected with a twinkle in his eyes. "You're just assertive."

Audrey arched an eyebrow. "Are you making fun of me?"

"Would I do that?"

"Absolutely. Rogues do whatever they like."

Blake shook his head sorrowfully. "Not whatever they like. I've been wanting to hold you all afternoon."

Audrey's heartbeat fluttered wildly. "What stopped you?"

He reached out to run a finger along her cheek, then stopped in midair and shook his head. He pulled his hand away. "The look in your eyes. It's still there. You're still afraid of me and I can't figure out why."

"It's not you exactly. It's what you represent."

"That powerful, domineering male type you're afraid of."

"Don't forget arrogant and self-confident."

"I'm not always so self-confident, Audrey. In fact, right now, I feel like an uncertain teenager on a first date. I haven't felt that way in a very long time."

"How do you like it?"

"I don't."

"Then maybe you have some idea how I feel, when things seem to be slipping away from me."

"Is control so important?"

"Not over other people, Blake. Never that. Only over my own life and, yes, that's very important."

He nodded slowly. "After what you told me earlier, I can understand that. What do we do about it? How do I reassure you that I'll always let you be your own person?"

"I don't know. Time, maybe. You can't expect me to trust you completely after knowing you for less than a day."

"We'll have to figure out something, because I have no intention of letting you get away and I'm not even sure how much time I can give you. I want you now."

He spoke so solemnly and with such certainty that Audrey felt her heart go still again. There was no answer she could give him and none was really even called for. Blake had simply made a declaration of intent and, while she could warn him away again, she knew now it would do no good. He'd made some sort of decision and he would go after her now with the same sort of single-minded determination that he'd used to make a failing winery a resounding success.

"Maybe we should get some sleep," he said softly. The simple suggestion, coming so soon after his vow to have her, carried a multitude of implications.

"They're bound to be out early looking for us," he added, when she said nothing.

The dying embers of the camp fire were red sparks against the night's darkness, giving off barely enough light for Audrey to see Blake's features. There was a decidedly hopeful gleam in his eyes that set off a wildfire of conflicting emotions inside her.

"No," she said abruptly.

Blake watched her closely. "Are you just being stubborn again?"

"Of course not," she denied.

"Aren't you tired, after the day we've had?"

"Not a bit," she lied boldly, trying to smother a telling yawn before he caught her.

"Well, I have to admit, I'm pretty beat," he said.

The air throbbed with tension.

"Fine. I'll just sit here and watch the fire a little longer. Don't worry about me."

"Audrey, you're going to get cold," he said, his voice edgy with impatience. She could see him struggle as he tried to temper his tone. "If we curl up here together, we'll be able to keep each other warm."

He made it sound perfectly innocent and logical, but logic had nothing to do with the frisson of excitement that played along her spine. *Curl up together*...dear heaven!

"Not a good idea."

"You're being foolish. We've just been all through this. Nothing will happen unless you want it to."

Exactly, she thought. That was the problem. She wanted it to. If she curved her body along the length of Blake's, she might as well kiss her resistance goodbye. She doubted if there was a woman with blood in her veins who'd be able to say no with his compelling masculinity stretched out beside her. And she just knew those powerful arms would be around her. Where else would he put them? He wasn't likely to spend the night with his hands tucked in his pockets. Even with the best intentions in the world, those hands of his were going to find their way to her flesh, even if they had to remove several layers of clothing to get there.

Worse, she wouldn't stop them.

"Blake, you're living in a dreamworld if you think you and I can just curl up together and nod off like a couple of innocent kids," she snapped. Frustration was making her even more tense than she had been before night had fallen and surrounded them with its intimate cloak of silence.

"We're mature adults," he retorted. "Not a couple of adolescents on the make. I can control my sexual appetites. Can't you?"

"Of course."

"Well, then?"

"Oh, just shut up and go to sleep."

"If that's the way you want it," he said. She heard him chuckling softly as he settled himself on the ground. "Sweet dreams, Audrey."

"Good night." The words whispered barely louder than a sigh past trembling lips.

Audrey stared at the red glow of the fire and tried to ignore the presence of Blake less than a foot away. With her legs drawn up to her chest, she rested her cheek on her knees.

It had been one hell of a day. She'd learned a lot about herself, thanks to Blake's prodding and the circumstances that had plunged them into this unexpected camping trip. She had a whole lot more resilience than she'd ever imagined. She was actually capable of being feisty, when it was necessary. What else had Blake called her? Assertive. Determined. She tried all of the words on for size and found they fit more aptly than she'd given herself credit for.

Had she always been that way or was there something special about Blake that had brought it out? Perhaps he'd just made her more aware of her own strengths, put her in situations that required brave responses. Perhaps that inner strength had been there all along, buried under a ton of emotional garbage heaped on her by Derek.

As the fire died out, the damp chill penetrated her clothing. Sleep had not eluded Blake as it was eluding her. He was breathing deeply and evenly, the sleep of a man who had nothing on his conscience. She thought there might be a certain amount of irony in that. Unlike the way she'd lived her life, Blake was a man who did what he wanted with no regrets. Even though he'd admitted that his methods of capturing her

today had been less than honest, he was the type
of man who felt the admission and his apology
put the matter to rest. Since he'd never intended
her any real harm, he couldn't imagine what all
the fuss was about. Audrey wished she had a
little more of his audacity, but maybe that would
come in time, too.

"If I keep hanging out with him, maybe a
little of it will rub off," she murmured, the
softly spoken words causing Blake to stir restlessly. She shivered and wished she hadn't been
quite so hasty in turning down his offer to keep
her warm.

Enviously, she watched him sleeping soundly
beside her. He was stretched out on his back,
open and vulnerable. She studied the muscular,
warm length of him and finally took a deep
breath.

"Why not?"

She inched herself closer, until her hip was
next to his. Then with the utmost care not to
disturb him, she lay down beside him, her head
resting on his outstretched arm. Turning sideways, she nestled against him, relishing the heat
emanating from his body.

Within seconds, though, once his warmth had
stolen over her, she felt something else stir deep

inside. An aching yearning began to build, just as Blake moaned softly and shifted positions, his arms coming around her, one leg dropping heavily across hers to entrap her.

Tension coiled inside her as her body burned with desire. There wasn't one square inch of her flesh—clothed or not—that wasn't sensitive to his proximity. On fire now from the inside out, Audrey perversely wanted him to wake, to complete this union that some part of her had known was inevitable from the moment they'd met.

But Blake slept on, and eventually, relaxing into his gentle possessive embrace, she did, too.

was such an intriguing bundle of contradic-
tions—fragility tempered by steel. He was lured
by her hidden strengths and wry humor, even as
he was taunted by her vulnerability and delight-
ful flashes of temper.

Blake's experience with women had included
an array of personalities, from bold and flashy
to domestic, from sleek and sophisticated to se-
rene and gentle. Each type had brought something special into his life, however fleetingly, but
no one of them had had the unique combination
of traits he'd found in Audrey. None of them
had touched his soul and, in the end, he'd remained alone.

Now he felt as though he'd found the one
woman who could bring spirit and joy into his
life, but she was filled with self-doubts. He had
encountered feminine insecurities in the past and
found them difficult to handle. They often led to
unreasoning jealousy that, in the end, destroyed
the relationship. Audrey's insecurities, though,
seemed to be of a different sort. He didn't know
what to make of them, even though her revela-
tions about her upbringing made things clearer.

Still, how did you go about convincing a
woman that she was more than capable of holding her own in any battle you were likely to

have? He didn't doubt for a minute that Audrey would always know her own mind and express her opinions vocally, that she would be as assertive as the situation warranted.

But she would also always be a soft touch and that, perhaps, was the real issue. She saw it as a problem. He didn't. In just the past twenty-four hours, he'd seen that she had a good and caring heart. She'd never said a single word condemning Harvey for interfering with her vacation plans. Nor had she even mentioned that it was because of Joe's desire to stay with his pregnant wife. Harvey had explained Joe's problem to Blake, but Audrey hadn't mentioned any of it. Blake knew that she would always be there for her friends without complaint. He thought that was a trait to be admired. Somehow, though, experience had taught Audrey that such caring and selflessness were weak, and she seemed determined to harden herself. He would have to prove to her how wrong that would be. That gentle souls were a rarity to be treasured.

She stirred restlessly in his arms and her eyes fluttered open. She gazed at him, glanced at her surroundings, then blinked in confusion.

"Morning, sweetheart," Blake murmured.

"Where am I?" she mumbled groggily as she tried to struggle free of his embrace.

"At least you're not asking who I am. It would be a terrible blow to my ego." He barely restrained an urge to laugh at her still puzzled frown. "Are you always this muddled in the morning or should I start worrying about amnesia?"

"Huh?"

"The balloon," he prodded.

"Oh." She closed her eyes again. "I forgot. The balloon fell down."

"We landed it," he corrected indignantly.

"In the rain."

Blake felt as though he were leading someone delicately back to reality. "That's right."

"It's not raining now?"

"No. It's morning and the sun is out."

"How early?"

"Does that matter?"

"It could explain why nothing makes sense to me."

"I see. You're not so terrific with mornings."

"I don't believe in them."

"Then it's probably better if you don't know what time it is."

She moaned and curled sleepily back against

him. This time it was Blake who groaned. He knew she had no idea what she was doing, that it would be a lousy thing to do to take advantage of her when she was half-asleep, but...

Breaking every vow he'd made to her, he leaned down and brushed a kiss lightly across her lips. Startled, wide-awake eyes met his.

"It works," he said, sounding pleased.

"What works?" she asked, instantly more alert and very suspicious.

"I always wondered if the Prince really could wake up Sleeping Beauty with a kiss."

Audrey pressed a hand over her eyes. "Do we really have to start the morning by testing fairy tales? Couldn't you just wait for me to wake up naturally?"

"I could, but we might have company before then."

"Company?"

"I expect John will have a rescue team looking for us soon."

She nodded agreeably and settled back down. "Fine. Wake me when they get here."

"Wouldn't you rather wake up now and take advantage of this lovely dawn?"

She peered at him balefully out of one eye.

"You're really not going to let me go back to sleep, are you?"

His fingers traced the curve of her brow, then caressed her cheek. "I'd rather be making love with you."

Her breath caught in her throat. "Blake..."

"How do you feel about that?"

"I'm not sure."

He followed the outline of the design on her sweatshirt with his finger, lingering where her breasts were rising and falling.

"What position?" he murmured.

She stared back at him in confusion. "You want to know what position I want to make love in?"

"Actually I was referring to your position on the company softball team, but I'll take a response to either question."

"Cute, Marshall."

"It was just a diversionary tactic." His gaze raked over her, taking in the sleepy, sexy eyes, the soft, creamy skin. He smiled. "But, yes, very cute."

His lips touched hers gently in subtle supplication. Her mouth was warm, soft and pliant beneath his. The kiss was so alluring that, once there, he couldn't go. His tongue persuaded until, breathless, she was kissing him back. The sweetness of it turned his blood to liquid fire.

He rolled her on top of him, his arms holding her loosely, allowing her the freedom to leave him, if that was her choice.

But she stayed—her hands caught in his hair, her mouth hot and hungry against his lips, his cheeks, mindless of the roughness of his overnight beard. His hands slid up under her sweatshirt and felt the muscles in her warm, bare shoulders tighten beneath his touch. Her T-shirt kept him tantalizingly removed from the curve of her spine as he ran his fingers to the dip at her waist. His fingers were trapped by the waistband of her jeans, so he began the upward caresses again, seeking the heat and friction of cloth against flesh that made her tremble. His thumbs ran along her ribs until they reached the swell of her breasts, finding the tips already so taut and sensitive that his slightest touch brought forth a low gasp of startled pleasure.

Her hips, pressed against his throbbing desire, stirred restlessly, creating an aching torment just shy of demand. He knew at once, then, the mistake he'd made. A few more minutes of this and his control would vanish. He would take her here and now in a blaze of wild abandon and she would let him. She would give in to the glorious sensations that had tempted them from the moment they'd met, but would she truly be giving herself, completely and without regrets? And did he want her without that?

Her lips burned against his neck. Her tongue cooled in turn and inside there was raging fire. Dear Lord, how he wanted her, needed her...but for more than this moment. Perhaps even forever.

With a low groan, he held her still, his hand stroking her back, gentling now, rather than inflaming.

"I'm sorry," he said softly, his breathing still ragged. "This isn't such a good idea."

Audrey went limp in his arms and heaved a sigh. Of regret? Or relief? He wasn't sure.

"Can't make up your mind?" she taunted, her own breathing uneven, but her tone light and bantering. She tried to untangle their legs, but he stilled her.

"Oh, I know what I want," he said, his voice thick with raw emotion. "I'm just not sure you do."

The silence that greeted his remark seemed endless, but at last she whispered against his cheek, "Thank you."

He hugged her reassuringly and wondered if he'd live to regret the depth of his willpower. "We will make love, you know."

"I know."

"Soon."

"I know that, too. Thank you for waiting."

"I will never take anything from you that you're not ready to give. Never."

He thought he felt a tear fall against his cheek, but he held her close and when he finally let her go much later, her eyes were bright and the brilliance of the smile she gave him was enough to make his heart sing. Mild regrets were nothing compared to the joy of that smile.

"I don't suppose you brought along eggs and bacon and pancakes?" she said cheerfully.

"Afraid not. I didn't expect this to turn into an overnight trip. How do you feel about champagne for breakfast?"

"Sounds pretty decadent."

"Is that a yes?"

She grinned at him. "Of course."

They drank to the dawn, as they had to the sunset, then Audrey gazed directly into his eyes with a look that could have started a forest fire. He swallowed uneasily. He didn't trust that look one bit. He had a feeling she was testing her newfound power over his senses.

"What are you thinking?"

"I was just wondering if perhaps that raging river weren't nearby."

"It should be a mile or so from here. Maybe less. Why?"

"How about a morning swim?"

"Where did this energy come from all of a sudden? Less than twenty minutes ago you could barely string three words together."

"No energy," she said, then added with deliberate innocence, "I just realized I'd never gone skinny-dipping in a river before. I might not ever get another chance."

Blake's eyes blinked wide and he stared at her. "Skinny-dipping?" he repeated huskily. "You mean you want to go swimming with me with no clothes on? What would your mother think?" He caught her determined expression. "Never mind. That's the point, isn't it?"

She grinned at him with the carefully calculated look of a wanton imp and shrugged. "You can stay here, if you'd prefer."

"Oh, no. I think I'll come along for this."

Blake's pulse was leaping erratically as they walked toward the river. What on earth was the woman trying to do to him? He'd only barely restrained himself earlier. The two of them stark naked in a river ought to be a test for sainthood.

"Are you really sure you want to do this?"

"Absolutely."

They found the stream about five minutes later. Audrey stopped in her tracks and stared at it in consternation.

"It isn't very deep."

"I told you that yesterday. It's probably not much more than knee-high."

Hesitant violet eyes met his and faltered. "Maybe this wasn't such a good idea."

"Why not?" Blake asked, beginning to unzip his windbreaker. Audrey's eyes followed his movements with fascination. "It's clear. It might be pretty cold, but we'll hardly notice once we get in."

He stripped off his windbreaker, then lifted his polo shirt over his head and heard her muffled gasp. "Come on, now. This was your idea."

"A bad one," she muttered nervously, backing up as his fingers went to the snap on his jeans. Her eyes were round as they watched him. "Definitely a bad one."

Suddenly Blake's shoulders shook with laughter. Audrey's eyes immediately narrowed and she glared at him.

"You knew this was going to happen, didn't you?"

"What?"

"You knew this water wouldn't come up to the chest of a three-year-old and you knew I was going to chicken out."

"It did occur to me that you were setting yourself up for a mighty big risk for a proper young lady."

Audrey's eyes flashed angrily at his words. "Now you're saying I'm a coward again."

"No, really. I swear it." Somehow the laughter didn't add to his credibility. He could see that in her eyes. Those glints of anger were coming back. "I just meant that skinny-dipping didn't seem to be your style."

"And just what do you think my style is? Boring? Uninteresting? Staid?" She tugged her sweatshirt over her head. "Okay, Mr. Macho, I'll show you."

"Audrey, wait. You don't have to prove anything to me."

She kicked off her shoes and stomped toward the stream, the sway of her rear end deliberately taunting him. At the last instant she stripped off her T-shirt. There was no bra, he realized, his gaze riveted to her bare back. Then her jeans and briefs were tugged off in a gesture that made up in speed what it lacked in grace. She never once looked back.

"I have to prove it to me," she muttered stubbornly and waded into the water.

It was entirely likely they could have heard her screech back in Aspen. "C-c…c-c…cold." Her teeth were chattering.

Blake stood on the edge of the bank and looked on helplessly, trying to keep his eyes averted from the sheer perfection of her curves. If this was a test for sainthood, he'd never pass. "Audrey, please, come out of there before you catch pneumonia. We don't have any towels."

"C-c…come and g-g…get me."

"Audrey!"

In a concession to modesty that turned her lips blue, she sat down in the middle of the stream and glowered at him. He could see the goose bumps from twenty feet away. Stubborn. Barely five feet tall and stubborn as any mule.

"Okay, dammit." He strode toward her, splashing in the shallow water, soaking his shoes and pants. "You are the most obstinate, pig-headed—"

"Assertive?" Suddenly she grinned at him.

He lifted his eyebrows in mocking agreement. "Assertive woman I have ever met." He scooped her into his arms and carried her back to shore. "And if you ever do anything that foolish just to prove a point again, I will tan your hide."

She poked him in the chest. "Don't even think about it."

He glanced down into her flashing eyes—he didn't dare look lower—and shook his head. "Has it occurred to you that you have a perverse streak in you that could drive a man to madness?"

"Really?" There was an interested gleam in her eyes.

"Don't let it go to your head. I didn't mean it as a compliment."

"That's okay. I consider it one. Now put me down so I can put my clothes on. I'm frozen clear through."

"Little wonder."

"Put me down and turn around."

"Audrey!"

"Blake!"

Blake plopped her unceremoniously on the ground and turned his back.

"This is ridiculous, you know. It's a little late for the shy maiden routine."

"A gentleman wouldn't think so." Her teeth were still chattering, and he whirled back around impatiently, just in time to see her tugging her sweatshirt back into place.

"Sit," he said gruffly. She gave him a mutinous look, but she sat. He knelt down beside her and picked up one dainty, ice-cold foot and rubbed it gently until the circulation was restored. Then he massaged the other one, his fingers lingering on her ankle where a pulse was beating rapidly. Finally, reluctantly, he released her foot and slipped on her shoes.

He tried very hard not to notice that his actions were having a decided impact on her breathing. If he thought about that, it might lead him to try massaging other parts of her chilled anatomy and then they'd be right back in the same tempting situation they'd been in earlier. It would be far better for the two of them if they didn't touch each other, not until they meant to follow through. A shudder rippled through him at the image that aroused. God help them both, if that didn't happen soon.

"We'd better get back to the balloon," he

said gruffly. "They should be looking for us by now."

They had just reached the edge of the clearing when they heard the drone of the helicopter overhead. Blake waved and it circled the clearing, then set down in the middle.

The blades of the helicopter had barely stopped whirling when, to his surprise, Harvey's hefty form appeared in the doorway. His hair was rumpled, his clothes bedraggled and there were dark circles under his eyes, but there was no mistaking the energy behind his fury. Blake had never seen the man so irate. He strode toward the two of them like some of avenging angel, waving a handful of newspapers in their direction.

Blake caught Audrey's eyes and winked. "I don't think the coverage was what Harvey expected when he sent you up here."

"I'll bet it was front page, though," she retorted with a grin. "That ought to count for something."

Blake glimpsed Harvey's expression again and shook his head. "I don't think so."

"Are you two out of your ever-loving minds?" Harvey blustered breathlessly. "Not only have you taken ten years off my life—years

I'd been counting on, I might add—but you've been made out to be no better than a couple of irresponsible teenagers. To tell you the truth, I think the press has been too kind. Of all the simpleminded, harebrained things to do.''

"We didn't plan on the storm," Blake pointed out.

"This mess started long before the rain. I've heard all about it, starting last night on the network news. You!" He thrust an accusing finger in Blake's direction and glowered at him. "I might have expected something like this from you."

Then he scowled ferociously at Audrey. "But I thought you were a smart lady. Tough, no-nonsense, businesslike. That's why I sent you up here, to keep him under control. I figured if anybody could handle him, you could. Instead, you let this overgrown playboy talk you into going for a joyride in some flimsy contraption that the devil himself wouldn't fly."

"I was kidnapped," Audrey said primly in response to Harvey's indignation. She had to avoid Blake's gaze to keep from laughing.

Her announcement definitely took the wind out of Harvey. She could see him trying to process it and decide how the press would deal with that tidbit. Apparently he didn't like what he saw. He sank down on a boulder and stared up at the two of them.

"Kidnapped?" he repeated dismally. "Dear God, Blake, of all the damn fool things to pull. Don't you have enough women in your life without going and kidnapping one of your own employees?"

"I only have one woman in my life," Blake said very, very quietly. "And I want to thank you for sending her to me. Otherwise yesterday might have been just another balloon race."

Harvey's eyes widened incredulously. "You're blaming me for this?"

"I'm not blaming you, Harvey. I'm thanking you. Can't you tell the difference?"

"I'm the one who's blaming you," Audrey inserted. "If you hadn't insisted on my coming up here this weekend in Joe's place, none of this would have happened. I'd be in Hawaii, Blake would have won the race, and you wouldn't have a public relations disaster on your hands."

"Wait just a minute. You are two grown people, even if you haven't been behaving much like it. You're responsible for your own destinies. This disaster is your doing, not mine. I was down in San Francisco doing my bit for the company by drinking wine that was no better than vinegar.''

He grimaced at the memory, then gazed suspiciously at Audrey. "Didn't you even try to stop him from kidnapping you?"

"Oh, I tried," she said. Blake nodded. Harvey stared at them in disbelief.

"You must not have tried very hard. I've heard you yell. If you'd done any of that, the police from four counties would have heard you."

"I yelled. Nobody seemed to take me seriously, least of all Blake." She shrugged. "Maybe a lot of his women yell."

Harvey's brows shot up. "Blake, is it? What happened to employee respect for the company president? What happened to Mr. Marshall?" He glared at Blake and added significantly, "Not that you deserve it."

"I told her she could drop it after I kissed her the first time," Blake said solemnly, but with a definite twinkle in his eyes.

That brought another horrified groan from Harvey. "Kissed her? You kidnapped her and then you seduced her? A sweet, innocent girl like Audrey?" he said incredulously. "I should have known the minute I heard the two of you were out in the middle of nowhere all alone that something like this would happen. That does it. I quit. Not even I can figure out how to handle this one.''

Blake sat down next to the distraught Harvey, placed an arm around his shoulder and squeezed. ''Come on now, Harvey. You don't really want to quit, do you? Think of this as a challenge, an opportunity. The company needs you.''

His voice dropped persuasively. He figured he'd better ooze sincerity or the best PR man in the business was going to walk out in a huff. ''I need you.''

Harvey accepted the flattery as his due. ''Damn right, you do. But I can't work for a man with the morals of an alley cat. Forget the company's image for the moment. How will I explain this little escapade of yours to Audrey's mother? She's a nice, middle-class, church-going lady, who raised her daughter for a better fate than this.''

''Right. Embroidering samplers,'' Blake grumbled under his breath.

Audrey didn't even hear him. She was regarding Harvey in confusion, trying to make sense of his reference to her mother. ''What does my mother have to do with anything? You don't even know her.''

"I do now. She's been on the phone with me all night. She's worried sick. She told me if anything happened to her daughter, it would be on my head. She sounded pretty convincing. I see now where you got your temper.''

"Terrific,'' she muttered.

"Some guy named Derek's been calling, too. He seemed real concerned.'' He studied her with renewed interest. "How come you've never mentioned him?''

A knot formed in her stomach and she ground out between clenched teeth, "Because there's nothing to say.''

Blake stared at her. "Derek's the jerk?''

She nodded.

"Okay,'' Blake said decisively. "That does it. Let's get in the copter and get back to Snowmass. Audrey can call her mother and reassure her and I'll deal with the press.''

"And what about this Derek?'' Harvey demanded.

"He can take a hike.''

"Sure, Blake, just dismiss him. You've gotten too damn sure of yourself. You make this whole thing sound perfectly simple,'' Harvey grumbled. "Exactly what do you plan to tell the media, when this guy goes to them and starts screaming about alienation of affection?"

"I don't think that will be a problem," Audrey said with wry conviction.

"I'm not so sure." He stared pointedly at Blake. "You will have to deal with the media, no matter what. What can you possibly say that won't make you look like the flake of the century?"

Blake gazed into Audrey's eyes—not Harvey's, she noticed—and said quietly, "I'm going to tell them I was up there falling in love."

Nine

Audrey wasn't sure whose gasp was more shocked, hers or Harvey's. Then she noticed the wily glint in Harvey's eyes. She'd seen that look before, usually when some outrageous promotional scheme was forming in his clever little mind. She had a pretty clear idea where this one was headed—to a church. More likely a cathedral, with her in satin and lace preceded by a line of bridesmaids that went on forever. Before she could get too attached to it, she tried to block the image of Blake in a tuxedo waiting for her at the end of the aisle.

"Forget it, Harvey," she said.

"But the man just said he's in love with you," he said, his enthusiasm making him speak in a run-together burst of words. He was practically rubbing his hands together at the prospect of all the plans to be made. "What could be more perfect than a wedding? If we play this right, hit hard on the romance angle, it'll get international media attention. You'll be on the cover of every magazine. The gossip columnists have been waiting for years for a story like this about Blake. You'll be the most talked-about bride since Fergie walked down the aisle in England."

"The 'romance angle,' as you call it, will get no media attention," she said adamantly as Harvey's enthusiastic expression dimmed. She was not stupid enough to believe he was ready to give up, so she armed herself for more. It took about ten seconds.

"But—"

"No, Harvey! Whatever there is between Blake and me—and I'm not saying there is anything—will remain between the two of us. Not even a tiny little hint about weddings, no leaks to your favorite reporters, nothing." She glanced from Harvey to Blake and back again. To her irritation, Blake's lips were twitching in amusement. He seemed to find her little display of assertiveness cute. She gritted her teeth.

"Is that clear?" she demanded. "I will not have my private life turned into a public spectacle."

"Your desire for privacy is all very nice, and under ordinary circumstances I'd agree with you," Harvey said, clearly trying to placate her. She'd heard that tone too often to be swayed.

"But these aren't ordinary circumstances," he reminded her. "We have a public relations crisis here for the company. We have to do something and do it quick."

"I don't care if the company drowns in a vat of its own wine," she muttered with feeling, before Blake's startled expression set her awash in guilt. "Sorry. I didn't mean that. Of course, I'm worried about the company's image."

She shot a pleading look at Harvey. This whole outrageous adventure was getting out of control. She might play along with Harvey's craziness once in a while, but she was not about to get married to keep a wine company afloat. Frankly, she thought he'd greatly exaggerated the depth of the crisis.

"Isn't there some other way?" she asked.

"I think I know one way we can avoid the whole thing," Blake said at last. "Come on. Let's get out of here. I'll explain in the chopper."

After directing several curious glances toward the arguing trio, John and the crew had busied themselves gathering up the balloon. Now John was waiting for them at the door of the helicopter.

"What are you going to do about today's competition, boss?"

Blake glanced at Audrey. "I think I'd better just drop out. There are things I need to take care of, and after yesterday it's a lost cause anyway."

"Blake, no," Audrey said, dismayed. "You can't do that." She looked at John. "Is there still time for him to get in the air this morning?"

"We've got the equipment at the rodeo grounds. They're only about halfway through the entries now. It won't take us long to get back. There should be plenty of time for him to launch. They'll probably make some allowances, given the circumstances."

"I'm dropping out," Blake said firmly, taking Audrey's hand and staring into her eyes. She was lost in that blue-eyed gaze, hardly hearing the rest of what he said. "If I stay around today, we'll never get away from the press. My whole idea was for the two of us to just disappear. My jet's at the airport. We could be away from Colorado in a matter of an hour or so. A day or two from now the story will die down."

Finally this so-called plan of his registered. A couple of years in public relations had taught her the folly of trying to ignore the press. "Blake, you're dreaming. If you just vanish, they'll only have more questions. They'll be like a bunch of bloodhounds on the scent of their prey."

"I don't much care if they have questions, as long as we're not around to answer them."

"Audrey's right, though," Harvey said, beaming at her approvingly. "Sooner or later they will find you. It'll be better if you give a few interviews today and then just get on with the competition. They'll admire you for sticking with it, fighting back against the odds and all that stuff. Everybody likes to be on the side of the underdog."

"But I want to keep Audrey away from the media. I don't want her to go through the third degree because of what happened." He studied her closely. "Wouldn't you rather we just got away from here?"

Her breath caught in her throat as his meaning sank in. She wasn't sure why it had taken it so long. He'd been emphasizing "we" for the past ten minutes. "You mean together?"

Blake nodded. "Of course."

She closed her eyes as if that would ward off the tantalizing possibilities that threatened to overwhelm her. It was wonderful of him to think of her, but hiding out together in some secluded place? It would never work. It would lead to trouble. Trouble, hell. It would lead to bed, no doubt about it.

"Blake, I need some space and you need to finish the competition. Running away will just…" She searched for the right word. "It will just complicate things."

"The competition be damned!" he exploded. "And I don't care about any complications, not for myself anyway. It's you I'm concerned about. If the press twists what happened between us into something tawdry, I want to be there for you. I don't want you forgetting for a minute that that's not the way it was."

She squeezed his hand and lowered her voice to a whisper that would exclude Harvey and the others, all of whom were watching them with fascination and clearly hanging on every word.

Whoever said women were the world's worst gossips had never met these men.

"I won't forget that," she promised. "Ever. How could I forget about learning to build a camp fire for the first time and skinny-dipping in an ice cold stream at dawn and waking up in your arms?"

He searched her eyes for what seemed to be an eternity. "Are you sure?"

"Very. Go out there today and win. Don't just turn the victory over to Larry Hammond, not when you could still take two events, today's and tomorrow's."

To her relief, he finally relented. "Where will you be, when I get finished this afternoon?"

Harvey, who had the sensitive ears of a forest creature and was clearly tired of being excluded, heard the softly spoken question and responded without hesitation. "She'll be back in California out of mischief."

Audrey's annoyance was evident in the scowl she directed at him. She was about fed up with Harvey's interference in her life. "Oh, no, I won't. You promised me a vacation in Aspen and I intend to hold you to it. I haven't hiked a single trail or seen the Maroon Bells or heard a concert. I am not leaving here until I have."

He seemed startled by her firm tone. Too startled. She realized she'd better start using it more often. "If you stay up here, the reporters are bound to track you down," he warned. "I won't be able to keep 'em away. You won't have a minute's peace."

"I can handle the reporters," she said valiantly. "You've taught me how. Besides, they're going to be much more interested in Blake than they will be in me."

Harvey's eyebrows rose. "You've got to be kidding. They're going to want to know all about the lucky mystery lady who was stranded for a night with the notorious and very eligible Blake Marshall."

"Well, they're going to be disappointed." She grinned at Blake. "I never kiss and tell."

He winked back at her, then his expression turned serious. "But you will stay? You won't let them frighten you away without talking to me first?"

"I'll stay." She had no idea why she felt so certain that waiting here with Blake was the right thing to do. It was every bit as dangerous as going into seclusion with him, but she knew she couldn't have done anything else. At the very least, she owed it to him to stick around and cheer him on for the remaining two events. At the most, they had fragile new feelings to explore.

Apparently Harvey had other ideas. As soon as the still reluctant Blake had been dropped off at the rodeo grounds, Harvey whisked Audrey away to his rental car, once again ignoring her protests.

"I always thought you were subtle, but you can be every bit as arrogant as Blake," she grumbled as he locked the car door and slammed it shut.

"I can be very pushy when it's called for," he agreed. "I'm surprised you haven't noticed that before."

That was the last thing he said as he drove her back to her motel. Throughout the short ride he maintained a tight-lipped silence.

"Look," she said at last. "I don't blame you for being furious with me at the way this turned out, but it wasn't my idea to come out here and it certainly wasn't my idea to go up in that blasted balloon. Maybe if you'd warned me about Blake, I would have known how to handle him. I tried to talk him out of dragging me along, but he isn't an easy man to convince. It was all pretty innocent, really. He seemed to have some crazy idea I'd enjoy the ride.''

"Yeah, I know. John Harley filled me in with as much as he knew.''

"Then what's the problem?''

He glanced over at her and, if anything, his lips compressed even more tightly. He shook his head.

"Come on, Harvey, spit it out. Something's on your mind.''

"Dammit, I'm worried about you,'' he finally growled.

She stared at him, stunned. "Me?''

"Yes, you. There's something going on here and I don't like it, in spite of that pretty little speech Blake made back there.''

"Less than an hour ago you were willing to give me away in marriage to the man.''

He had the grace to look guilty. "I got a little carried away. I'm sorry. That doesn't change the fact that you're no match for a man like him, Audrey.''

"Thanks,'' she grumbled.

He ignored her sarcasm and continued aiming low blows to her midsection. "Let's face facts. He travels in fast circles, too fast for you.''

Audrey swallowed another angry retort and

tried to deal with Harvey's burst of protectiveness rationally. "That's what I thought at first," she admitted quietly. "Now I'm not so sure. He's not at all the man I expected him to be. He's certainly not the man whose every romantic interlude is detailed in all the gossip columns. He has more substance than that. Just as important, I'm different when I'm with him. Tougher. More assertive. I think I like what he brings out in me."

Harvey tried another tack. "It's a lousy idea to go getting mixed up with your boss."

"*You're* my boss," she pointed out. "Not Blake."

"Stop splitting hairs. Blake pays the two of us and don't you forget it. I guarantee you he won't."

"If you're implying that he's going to take advantage of our professional relationship, then I think that's a crummy thing to say about both of us. Blake wouldn't try and I'd never let him."

"Sorry. It's just that I've always thought of you sort of like a daughter. I hate to see you getting mixed up with a man who'll walk all over you and leave you hurting. I agree with you that deep inside Blake's a decent enough man, but I don't know that he'll ever settle down."

"Who says I want him to?"

Harvey shook his head. "Oh, Audrey, who are you trying to fool? Me or yourself? I caught that look in your eyes back there. For all your objections, you're a woman with wedding bells ringing in her ears. Besides, settling down is what you deserve. I saw you down at Fisherman's Wharf with those kids a couple of weeks back. You were great with them. You should have a half dozen of your own. But, I'm warning you, that hearth and home bit isn't Blake. If you think you can tame him, you'll be in for some rocky times."

A tiny half smile formed on Audrey's lips as she recalled the conversation she'd had with Blake the previous day, his professed desire for just that sort of tame existence. "Apparently you don't know the man nearly as well as you think you do."

"Audrey, I've known him a long time now. I even admire him as a businessman. But I've known his type even longer."

"His type?" she said indignantly. "Just what is his type? That wealthy playboy facade he puts on for the public so we can sell more wine or the gentle, sensitive man who kept me from panicking when we had to land during that storm?"

"You would never have been out in that storm if that 'gentle, sensitive man' hadn't dragged you into that balloon. He didn't hesitate for a minute to just take what he wanted then, did he?"

Audrey sighed. "Okay. You have a point."

"Another point." Harvey was apparently keeping score and wanted to be sure she realized she was losing. She glared at him.

"Harvey, I'm not saying that the idea of getting involved with Blake doesn't scare the daylights out of me, because it does. But I'm beginning to think it's a risk worth taking. Besides," she added emphatically, "this is really none of your business."

"Suit yourself," he said as he pulled up behind her motel. "You're a big girl and I can't stop you. But if you come back to work sniffling and carrying on about what a creep he is, I'll see to it you do nothing but filing for the next six months."

She heard the gruff tenderness and concern in Harvey's voice and grinned. "Deal," she said as she dropped a light kiss on his cheek and slid out of the car. "By the way, am I officially on vacation now?"

He rolled his eyes. "Go. Enjoy. I'll go back

and deal with that pack of journalistic wolves at
the Balloon Festival.''

"Thanks, Harvey."

"Don't thank me yet. The jury's still out on
this mess. Think about what I've said."

By late afternoon Audrey was convinced that
the jury had come in with a guilty verdict—
against Blake. Surely the competition had ended
hours earlier, but there had been no call and no
sign of him. Determined not to sit around in her
room moping and wasting another minute of her
well-deserved vacation, she dressed in a floral-
patterned cotton skirt, a bright pink camp shirt
and sandals and set off for the main part of town,
thoroughly enjoying the friendly atmosphere of
Aspen, the patches of park, the sparkling foun-
tains, the crisp air.

With the sun shining brightly, the sidewalk
cafés along Cooper and Hyman avenues were
crowded and noisy. After window-shopping for
nearly an hour, Audrey chose one of the restaurants with an available outdoor table and settled
down with a glass of wine and a plate of nachos.
She watched the strolling families, the young
couples on bikes, the tanned women with long
legs and sun-streaked hair and arms laden with
packages and the sexy, well-built men in their

designer tennis shorts and matching shirts. She'd
never seen in one place so many obviously
wealthy people, people whose lives were marked
by class and sophistication, by personal fitness
trainers and face-lifts. These were people who'd
be at home on a ski slope here or in the casinos
of Europe or in a designer fashion salon in Paris.
She'd noted the prices in the windows of some
of the stores and she doubted if she spent in a
year what some of these people had just spent
in a single shopping spree.

Catching snatches of the conversations around
her, she found that there were physicians here
for conferences and musicians taking part in the
Aspen Music Festival. The talk ranged form sur-
gical procedures at one table to violin sonatas at
the next with a violent debate over an upcoming
tennis tournament at yet another. For such a
small town, which had been built up by the ex-
cellence of its facilities for skiing, Aspen had an
astonishing array of sports, as well as intellectual
and cultural activities to attract a well-to-do
summer crowd.

She found that she was fascinated by it all,
but not particularly envious that this wasn't her
natural environment. She had most of the things
she wanted in her life—dear friends, job security

in a stimulating atmosphere, a small savings account, the ability to travel occasionally. The only thing missing, really, was love. And now Blake had promised her that, if she wanted it, if she could accept such a gift, offered after so short a time, as real.

Acceptance was getting less and less likely with every minute that passed, however. She was beginning to feel abandoned, beginning to share Harvey's doubts and the wisdom of remaining. She wondered if Blake had called by now or if he was off again in pursuit of some other woman, some other challenge.

Suddenly a hand reached across the low railing that separated the café from the pedestrian mall. Familiar fingers picked up her glass and Audrey's gaze followed the disappearance of her wine until her eyes clashed with Blake's impudent face. His hair was still damp and unruly from his shower. He was wearing khaki shorts that revealed lean, muscular, perfectly formed thighs. His short-sleeved polo shirt was blue, just one shade darker than his eyes. The effect was casual. It was also overwhelmingly masculine. It took her breath away.

"Miss me?" he inquired, taking a sip of the

wine and promptly grimacing. "This isn't mine."

"Sorry. Yours wasn't on the wine list. Be thankful I didn't decide on Mexican beer."

With one quick move and no invitation, he had stepped over the railing and sat down across from her. He picked up a cold nacho and nibbled on it, making another face. "You haven't answered me yet. Did you miss me?"

She gave a deliberately exaggerated shrug. She would not give him a direct answer to that question, if he tortured her. Staring closely at the remaining nachos as if selecting one were an incredibly important decision, she said nonchalantly, "Why would I miss you? I've been busy shopping."

"I don't believe you."

"Why?"

"No packages."

"Ah." Damn.

"If you're going to try little white lies on me, don't make them so easy to check out," he warned with a twinkle in his eyes.

"I'll keep that in mind. How was the competition?"

"I won."

"Fantastic." Her excitement for him was genuine. "Does that keep you even with Hammond?"

"Yes. Tomorrow will break the tie."

He seemed surprisingly reticent, almost disinterested. Only yesterday this race had been the most important thing in the world to him. Now something else was clearly on his mind and she thought she had some idea what it might be. "How did it go with the reporters?"

He shrugged. "I gave them enough of a story to keep them happy, but I suspect they'll be back for more. Just as Harvey anticipated, they're all curious about the mystery woman who was with me."

Audrey grinned in spite of herself. "Don't you ever tell Harvey this, but I think I like the idea of being a woman of mystery."

"Do you really?" There was an odd note in his voice.

"Blake, is there something wrong?"

"You tell me."

"We're talking in circles here."

"Sorry. You're right. I'll be more direct. I thought you were going to wait for me."

"I did. Then I got hungry and I wanted to get in a little sight-seeing. How did you find me?"

He was twirling her wineglass around in nervous fingers. He seemed fascinated by the process. Finally, he looked up, his expression chagrined, and said, "You mean after I broke into your room and found out you hadn't left town after all?"

Audrey groaned and examined his face for some sign that he was joking. "Blake, you didn't."

He nodded seriously. "Oh, yes, I did. The motel manager was very understanding, though. I guess he must deal with a lot of crazy men in love. He's replacing the lock now, at my expense of course."

Her voice softened. "I told you I would stay."

"I know, but I was afraid Harvey might have talked you out of it. I panicked when I got there and you were gone."

"Harvey tried to talk me into going home."

"How come you didn't listen? I'm sure he mounted a very persuasive argument."

"Oh, he did. Told me all about what a rake you are."

"Didn't you believe him?"

"Absolutely. I had you pegged from the first, remember."

"But you stayed anyway." His lips curved in a pleased half smile.

"I wanted to."

"I'm glad." He studied her closely for several endless minutes, until she felt the blood rise in her cheeks. "Tell me something," he said finally. "I want you to think about it and be completely honest."

"Anything." Her heart hammered as she waited for the rest. He looked so serious all of a sudden.

"Am I just another risk you're determined to take?"

The question threw her. With a sudden flash of insight she realized it might be true, that Blake might be her way of trying to put the past at rest. How could it be anything more in so short a time? She wanted it to be, but she wasn't sure. How on earth could she explain that to him?

She didn't have to. Blake sighed at her hesitation. "I was afraid of that."

"No, Blake, really," she denied. "It's more than that. It's important. At least I want it to be. I just don't know exactly what it is yet. Love? Infatuation? A risk? I'm not sure. You, what's happening between us, it took me by surprise. I haven't had these feelings in a long time."

"You took me by surprise, too. I came up here with one thing on my mind and a little imp stole my heart instead."

"Now you tell me something. Is the pace going to change now that we're on the ground, maybe slow down a little so I can catch my breath?"

"Slow down?" he repeated incredulously, his mouth curving into a devilishly wicked grin that made her heart flip over. "No way. I'm going to be sweeping you off your feet."

"I thought we'd agreed that I need a little space," she said, an edge of desperation in her voice.

"A little, not the whole damn state. When you start feeling crowded, you say something and I'll give you room to breathe, but we're going to explore the feelings together, not from different places. Starting tonight..." He hesitated. "If you're ready."

She dared a glance straight into his eyes. To her relief that look of blazing, unrelenting desire was there again, as strong and clear as ever. It made her weak with longing. Suddenly getting some space didn't seem nearly so necessary or so attractive. She was drawn to Blake in ways that had little to do with rational thought and everything to do with powerful, compelling emotions that she no longer wanted to resist.

Before she could have any second thoughts, she said boldly, "Care to go back and see how they're coming with the lock on my room?"

Her voice shook, but this time it was Blake who seemed stunned into silence. "And?" he said cautiously.

"We can test it to make sure it works."

He sucked in his breath. Without another word and without taking his eyes from hers, Blake threw several crumpled bills, far more than necessary, on the table and took her hand. "Let's go."

He dropped her hand the instant they were on their way. It was as though he was afraid to touch her and, as they walked, his expression grew increasingly troubled. They were less than a block from the motel, the tension between them mounting, when he stopped and looked down at her. He took her chin between thumb and forefinger and tilted it up until he could read the expression in her eyes.

"If you didn't mean what I thought you meant back there, I may never forgive you." He tried to make a joke of it, but she could hear the strain and hope in his voice.

Audrey grinned at him impishly. "What did you think I meant?"

"That you wanted to make love."

"Perceptive man."

He released a ragged sigh and draped an arm around her shoulders. "Thank God."

Unfortunately, Harvey was sitting in the middle of Audrey's bed when they returned, newspapers scattered all around, a pair of scissors in his hand.

"Where the hell have you two been this time?"

Blake and Audrey exchanged a thoroughly frustrated glance.

"How did you get in here?" Audrey demanded.

"The manager said I could wait. He was here with some guy fixing the door." He gazed pointedly at Blake when he said it.

"Leave, Harvey," Blake said.

Harvey blinked up at them. "What?"

"You heard the man," Audrey concurred. "Out of here."

"But we need to talk strategy."

"We can talk strategy to your heart's content

some other time," Blake said. His voice rose imperiously. "Not now."

Harvey's eyes widened, then he took a really good look at Audrey, who was standing there feeling like an embarrassed schoolgirl caught necking by her parents. "Ohh," he muttered. "Sorry, I'll see the two of you later."

"In the morning, Harvey. At the festival site."

Grumbling under his breath, Harvey went to the door, then turned and scowled ferociously at Blake. "If you hurt her..."

He never finished, because Blake interrupted. "I won't hurt her, Harvey. That's a promise."

Ten

The minute the door closed behind Harvey, Audrey's heartbeat quickened. She wanted to call him back and ask him to stay for a drink, dinner, dessert, maybe even a late-night movie, anything to prevent her from being alone with Blake in this ugly room that suddenly seemed to be dominated by its queen-size bed. She heard the ticking of every one of her alarm clocks echoing in the thickening silence. Not one of those clocks was marking time as rapidly as her pulse.

Breathless, her eyes wide, she stared at Blake, tall and boldly handsome, filling the doorway

with impressive, barely leashed energy. What on
earth had she been thinking of when she'd bra-
zenly suggested they come back here? Surely
there were better, safer ways to test her emotional strength. She should never have picked a
pirate, a man who could steal her heart so easily
she'd wouldn't recognize the loss until it was far
too late.

But, God help her, she wanted him to touch
her, wanted her blood to slow and thicken into
sweetly throbbing torment.

Just as desperately she wanted to touch him,
to feel his muscles flex and tense under her caress, to have his ragged, desire-paced breath sing
its mating song in her arms. She wanted that
feeling of being spectacularly alive and one with
another person. This person. Whether her choice
or fate's, this was destined to be. Forever. For
now. Who could tell?

Admittedly, though, she was terrified by the
implications. This would be no casual fling, no
holiday affair that left her with memories but no
scars. She'd never been able to handle that sort
of thing anyway. Being with a man, loving him,
had always meant offering him her heart as well
as her body. Somehow, after all the months of
self-recriminations and pain after Derek, she

knew she was finally ready to do that with
Blake. In a very short time he had given her
back her self-respect, encouraged her attempts to
grow and be strong.

Though Blake had claimed to love her, she
wasn't sure he really wanted a lasting commit-
ment. Perhaps Blake was the kind of man who
gave love easily and just as easily took it away.

Knowing him for barely more than a full day,
even if they had been intimate, emotionally
grueling hours for her, was hardly a test of a
relationship's endurance. The real test would
come in the weeks and months to come, when
they were back in the real world of endless hours
on the job and responsibilities and other emotional ties.

Now, however, with Blake moving toward
her, his eyes blazing a seductive message, was
no time to be having second thoughts. For all of
its potential for heartache, she wanted this time
with Blake, wanted to discover if the warmth
and sensitivity could last, wanted the magic of
the past twenty-four hours to go on for as long
as it could. Yes, part of that was because she
wanted to take a risk, to prove to herself that she
was capable of loving again. She could only

pray that she wasn't being unfair to either one of them by asking so much of a single night.

"We should have champagne and roses and candlelight," Blake said softly. "I wanted to do this right, to make it special."

"That's not what makes it right and it is special. All those things are in my heart," she said candidly.

He stepped closer and his heat surrounded her, lured her like a candle's flame. She lifted a hand to his chest. The pounding of his heart beneath her touch gave her courage. His shirt collar was open and dark hairs glinting with golden highlights tempted her to press her fingers against flesh that burned hot beneath its rough, masculine covering. The pulse at the base of his throat beat furiously and his breathing grew uneven. But he stood patiently giving her time to make her choices, time to lead the way.

This time it was Audrey who moved closer, suddenly needing to touch her lips to the strong column of his neck. The kiss, combined with the clean scent of soap and his warm, musky scent, sent ripples of delight cascading through her. When she trembled, she put her hands on his shoulders to steady herself and found his muscles tight with the tension leashing both his considerable energy and his even more potent desire.

Shyly meeting his gaze, she found his lips parted, his eyes closed and a look of astonished pleasure on his face. She was responsible for that expression. The realization made her feel almost giddy with power and weak with relief. It gave her the much-needed boost of courage to stand on tiptoe and slant her mouth boldly across his, to run her tongue along his teeth, then dip inside when he gasped and held her close, his arms tightening possessively around her. The kiss deepened, became an urgent, breathtaking moment in time.

If the other kisses they had shared had been wonderfully exciting, this one was pure bliss, unfurling passion in gentle waves.

When the kiss ended at last, a mere pause in the promise of more, he said gently, "It's been a long time for you, hasn't it? This isn't something you do lightly."

She nodded.

He met her embarrassed gaze with tenderness and caring. "I know what you think about my reputation, but it's been a long time for me, too. Don't worry about anything. I'll protect you." His fingers grazed her lips as he vowed as well,

"I won't rush you, sweetheart. We have the rest of the night and more, if you need it."

"I need you now, Blake," she whispered, wondering if he could possibly know how true those words were, if he sensed the urgency that tore at her. She needed his loving, she needed him to make her forget the past, to bring her into the present, perhaps even to hint at the future. "Now, please."

He lifted her into his arms and carried her to the bed. When she reached for the buttons on her blouse, he stilled her fingers. "Let me."

One by one he slid the buttons free and as her shirt fell away from her flesh, his lips caressed, his tongue savored. Her body arched into his scorching touch, seeking a remembered pleasure, but finding something surprisingly new and better. The light burning brightly in his eyes revered her in a way that made her tremble with awe and humility that he could feel so much for her. That glint of primitive desire left her wondering how it could be that she'd never known that loving could be this gentle and yet so intense that it reached the core of her with its consuming, white-hot flames.

Clothing vanished, as if by magic, and Blake's hungry mouth and possessive touch

were everywhere. He stroked. He teased. He
massaged. Every caress was more devastating
than the last, until she was certain she would
shatter into a million pieces before he was done.
It was wonderful. Thrilling. But much too much.

She was vulnerable in a way she hadn't allowed herself to be since Derek. The memory of
the last time they'd been together—the shouted
accusations, the cruelty, so much worse because
it had come so unexpectedly—flitted through her
mind and left her suddenly cold and very, very
frightened.

*I won't let him do this to me. I won't. Blake
is different. We can be different.*

With a small cry she reached out to Blake,
drawing him closer, urging him to offer more of
those pleasure-pain kisses that made her breasts
achingly full and sensitive. She lifted his shirt
and ran her fingers over smooth, hot flesh and
corded muscles. In a single smooth gesture, he
pulled the shirt away. She had seen that bare
chest with its shadowed triangle of hair before,
had felt the wicked temptation to trace its path,
but it was nothing compared to the sensation of
knowing that she could do just that, that for tonight at least Blake was hers.

A thumb found the hard masculine nipple buried in a whorl of hair and stroked until Blake uttered a low groan. Then she sought out its mate and repeated the process until he was trembling beneath her touch. Her hands moved on, over his flat, taut belly, to the waistband of his khaki shorts. She hesitated at the snap and could feel Blake tense in anticipation. A faint smile formed on her lips and then she kept going, carefully, consciously avoiding the hard evidence of his arousal. He closed his eyes and moaned.

"Are you trying to torture me?"

As a response, she kissed the inside of his thighs, then each knee, as her nails raked along a similar path in a lightly teasing gesture.

"You are trying to torture me," he said in a raw-edged voice.

"I want to give everything to you. I want you to feel everything," she whispered.

"If I feel much more, we won't leave this bed for a month. Come back up here, where I can share it with you."

"Not yet. There's this one little place I haven't kissed yet." She ran her tongue along the arch of his foot. "And here's one more." Murmuring seductive little comments as she went, she worked her way back up his body until she could feel the coil of tension in his muscles, feel the heat radiating from him, see the sheen of per-spiration forming on his chest.

"Enough," he finally growled, turning her onto her back as he reached for the promised protection. Probing fingers caressed her moist-ness, building a new sweet tension in her. He poised on his knees over her, gazed into her eyes with a look that hinted of heaven. Then with a quick stroke, he was deep inside her, filling her, taking all the love she had to give.

He lifted her hips, penetrating more deeply in a slow mating that sent her senses reeling. She writhed under him, needing him, drawing him in, seeking the wild torrent of feelings that would split her apart. With each deep thrust, each touch of her swollen breasts, he carried her to the edge of ecstasy.

And each time she held a part of herself back, wouldn't let herself spin free into that whirlpool of sensations, couldn't give in to the shattering intimacy, the ultimate giving. There was wild-ness, but no abandon. She was digging her nails into his back, willing herself to let go, but it wouldn't happen. The peak was out there, just beyond her reach.

When Blake exploded inside her at last, her name a harsh cry on his lips, she felt an instant's joy at his pleasure, then an awful, numbing emptiness. She went perfectly still beneath him and turned her head into the pillow, trying to hide the tears of anger and frustration that came with the discovery that after Derek, she was incapable of loving, of sharing in the bliss.

After several minutes, she sensed that Blake was watching her. She met his troubled gaze, then glanced away, feeling an incredible, overwhelming guilt.

"This wasn't good for you, was it?" he said softly, his fingers tracing the dampness on her cheeks. The wistful, lost look in her eyes tore at his insides. How could something that had brought him so much pleasure leave her looking so terribly alone?

"Yes. It was wonderful."

She said it valiantly, but she couldn't keep her lips from trembling. The facade scared him more than her tears. It was the beginning of a wall, a wall that could only go higher unless he battered it down now.

"Sssh." He pressed a finger against her mouth to prevent another denial. "No lies, Audrey. There will never be any lies between us, not even the tiny white ones meant to protect."

She pulled herself free from his embrace and

clutched a pillow in front of her. She held it tightly, as though it were all she had in the world to cling to. *Hold me like that*, he wanted to shout. *Share this with me, whatever it is. Explain your pain.*

But he sensed she couldn't—yet. With the intuition of a man in love and just beginning to understand the intricacies of his beloved's mind, he knew there were ghosts in this bed with them. What he didn't know was how to exorcise them.

"I'm sorry," he apologized. "I rushed you into this."

She lifted her chin and he grinned at the sign of stubbornness. "That's very gallant, but I'm the one who dragged you back here, remember."

"I could have said no."

His words brought on a tentative smile. "Don't tell me my bad habits are rubbing off on you."

"That, my love, is not the point. I should have realized it was too soon. No matter what my feelings are for you and what I think yours are or will be for me, trust comes less quickly. You still have some scars and only time and trust are going to erase them. Making love is the ultimate test of trust."

She bit her lip, then gazed at him through half-lowered lashes. "Do we have time?"

"What kind of a question is that?"

"I mean after what happened..." Her voice trailed off uneasily.

"Don't you ever dare be ashamed or embarrassed by what happened tonight. We made love in every sense of the word. You and me."

"But I didn't...I couldn't..."

"You will," he reassured her, sliding his arms around her. He buried his lips in her hair and sighed. "I believe that with all my heart. You seem to think this was all your fault, but it wasn't. It was mine for pushing you into something before you were ready, for not taking more time with you. That won't happen again. I've told you before and I meant every word: we have all the time in the world to find our way together."

He could feel the tension ease out of her as she relaxed in his embrace. Slowly, the knot in his own stomach came untied and he felt hope stir again.

"Now, I have a plan," he announced before the reality sank in that he was holding the woman he was crazy about naked in his arms. That would change his plan dramatically and wouldn't be wise at all. She clearly viewed to-night as some sort of failure, and he had no intention of setting her up for another one.

"If we hurry," he said, "we can pick up some food and go over to the music tent. I saw the schedule earlier and it's a jazz concert."

"We don't have tickets."

"I'm sure we could get them, but for what I have in mind, we won't need them."

"I'm almost afraid to ask, but what do you have in mind?"

"I was thinking we should keep up with our family tradition."

"Family? Tradition? We haven't known each other that long."

"Ah, but the very best traditions can get started in no time."

"And what exactly is this tradition of ours?"

"A picnic under the stars, of course."

"Do you have something in particular against the food in restaurants?"

"Not at all. Many restaurants have very fine chefs. I always get them to pack my picnics."

Laughter bubbled up and that haunted look left Audrey's eyes at last. "I see. It's the confinement you don't like. Walls, ceilings, things that keep out wind and rain."

"And stars," he noted. "Don't forget they also keep out stars and breezes and the scent of pine. Now, you just think about that, while I take my shower and get dressed. Then I'll go find us the best meal in Aspen, while you get ready."

Filled with renewed energy, he jumped out of the rumpled bed and headed for the shower, just as Audrey inquired with an unexpected edge of irritation, "Is there any point in my arguing?"

He stopped just inside the bathroom and stared back at her, puzzled by the hint of exasperation he'd heard. "Do you want to?"

She chuckled then and threw up her hands in a gesture of resignation. "I suppose not. It was just token resistance. Sometimes this assertiveness kick of mine gets out of control."

"You can practice on me all you like, just be sure to give me a clue when you're really serious. I'd hate to have you slam me over the head with a bottle of my cabernet sauvignon, just because we got our signals crossed."

"Unfortunately, sometimes I'm not so sure myself. I'll have to work on that. It'd be a shame to tell you no, when I mean yes."

"You've got that right," he said, grinning wickedly. He closed the bathroom door, then opened it again. "Care to join me in the shower?"

"And miss this gourmet picnic?"

"Right. Priorities are important. Picnic first, a togetherness shower later." He winked at her. "Count on it."

Eleven

"This isn't like any picnic I ever saw," Audrey said as she pulled two outrageously expensive, fine bone china plates from a picnic hamper that was so cumbersome and heavy that even Blake had struggled to carry it from the car.

After carefully depositing the plates on the blanket, she held up a fork and examined it in the mauve shadows of twilight. "Sterling silver, huh? Whatever happened to plastic?"

"Tacky." Blake wrinkled his nose.

"But disposable."

"Chef Luis would faint at the prospect of his

food being eaten with plastic utensils, even though I'm sure the main course will be so tender it wouldn't matter.''

Audrey shook her head, then drew a crystal goblet from the basket and stared at him in dismay. ''Waterford? Blake, do you have any idea how expensive this is? It's breakable, too.''

''That only matters, if we decide to throw it against a tree to solemnize a toast.'' He grinned at her suggestively. ''Do you have one in mind?''

She rolled her eyes at his audacity. ''Doesn't money mean anything to you?''

His eyebrows rose. ''Does it to you?'' His words were weighty with significance.

She shot him an indignant look. ''Of course not. I meant the opposite. Why are you wasting it on fancy frills like this?''

''A frill is something superfluous,'' he protested. ''I don't consider serving you an elegant meal in a lovely setting a waste of my money. You deserve to be treated like a lady. You will have nothing but the best to show you how much I care about you.''

Her eyes grew misty as Blake's words flooded her with warmth. It was such a contrast to the past, when she'd been doing all the giving. Perhaps it was time she learned to accept things graciously.

Blake must have sensed she was about to burst into tears, because he said briskly, "Now stop grumbling before the food gets cold. Chef Luis gets very testy, if his meals aren't served properly. It ruins the subtle bouquet of the spices or something."

"What kind of food does this chef of yours prepare that it has to be treated so gingerly?"

"Mexican," he said, opening a container of guacamole salad and waving it under her nose.

"Mexican?" she repeated incredulously. "You can get good Mexican at a fast food place with paper plates and plastic forks."

"Not as good as this, I guarantee you." He lifted the foil off a container of beef burritos, smothered in *picante* sauce and sour cream. "See what I mean."

The minute the aroma reached her nose, Audrey's mouth watered and she stretched out a hand. Blake brushed it aside. "Oh, no, you don't. Hand me one of those plates. You are not eating this out of the pan."

"Old habits die hard," she retorted. "I swear to you it will taste just as good and I won't be terrified of chipping it and costing myself two months salary.''

Blake held the burritos just beyond her reach. "Do we need to have a serious talk about money? You seem hung up about it.''

"Mine," she asserted. "Not yours. You can have all you want. I don't happen to have as much.''

"Then let me spend mine in a way that pleases me. I will gladly pay for any plates you chip.''

Before she could come back with a retort, he popped a forkful of the burrito into her mouth. Any temptation she might have felt to spit it back out in a gesture of protest died the moment the spicy flavorings hit her tongue. Yes, it was definitely time to accept things graciously. The shredded beef had just the right combination of cumin, onions and garlic. There was a sharp bite to the picante sauce and the sour cream provided a cooling contrast. It was heavenly and it didn't matter a hoot anymore that she was eating it with silver so elegant it could have been on the table for a formal state dinner at the White House.

"Wonderful," she murmured, cautiously accepting the china plate from Blake.

He nodded in satisfaction. "I think I've found one way to shut you up," he said.

"I didn't know that was one of your goals."

"It only crosses my mind when you go into one of your stubborn acts. Food and kissing seem to be effective counterattacks," he said, then peered at her thoughtfully. "I wonder if there are any others. I may need a more complete arsenal over the years."

Over the years. Nice phrase, she thought, as her pulse skipped happily. But then Blake was a sensitive man. If she'd doubted it when they met, she certainly didn't now, not after what he'd done for her tonight.

Not once since they left the motel had he mentioned what had happened between them in that room. Not once had he been anything but kind and gentle after she had withheld that final gift of herself. Perhaps it had been at that moment, when she had been sitting naked and shivering and embarrassed and he had apologized to her, perhaps it had been then that she had truly fallen in love. Dear heaven, let him be as patient as he was caring!

He tapped the edge of her plate with his fork to get her attention. "You're not eating."

"I guess my mind wandered."

His eyes narrowed and he touched her chin. "No unhappy thoughts tonight. Promise?"

He'd done it again. He'd read her mind and tried to take away the hurt. Audrey blinked back a fresh batch of tears. She gave him a faltering smile. "Promise."

The whispered word was virtually drowned out by a crescendo of sound from the music tent. As night fell, trumpets and saxophones and, astonishingly enough from a jazz band, violins filled the air with a joyous, lively beat that had her tapping her toes. Haunting melodies followed, then intricate pieces with solos that were wild and uninhibited.

Lying back on their blanket, the stars bright above them, the aspens whispering in the breeze, Audrey was utterly at peace, lost in the music. Each song affected her in a different way, lifting her up, taking her down, playing her heart like one of the orchestra's instruments. It was the clear, high, rippling notes of a flute, rising over a background of subtle rhythms, that made her tremble so that Blake pulled her into his arms and held her tight. When the concert ended, she felt drained and deliriously happy all at once.

"That was wonderful," she said with a sigh.

Oblivious to the people pouring from the music tent, Blake lowered his face to hers and kissed her, a slow, lingering, tender kiss that made music soar again, this time deep inside.

"I love watching you," he said, gazing down into her eyes. "I think that's what I first noticed about you, the delight you take in everything. It's like watching a child when he first becomes aware of the world around him. Every discovery brings such amazement. Don't ever change. Don't become jaded and cynical."

"Have you known a lot of cynical women?"

"Too many. They live too fast, get hurt too often and pretty soon they're hard or pretending to be. Sometimes it scares me that you might be trying to do the same thing, to protect yourself from another hurt."

"No one likes to be hurt," she said defensively.

"No, but there are better ways of handling it than shutting yourself off from the world. In the long run that's the greatest hurt you can suffer. Taking chances may bring you pain, but it's also the only way you'll ever find real happiness."

His hand ran along the curve of her hip and lingered on her thigh. For Blake it seemed a casual, almost unconscious gesture, but it stirred Audrey's blood again.

"Enough philosophizing for tonight," he said. "Let's get you back to your motel. I have another competition in the morning."

"I suppose it's at dawn again."

He grinned. "Absolutely. Do you plan to be there?"

"That all depends."

"On what?"

She took a deep breath and said, "Whether you plan to stay tonight to make sure I wake up."

He seemed to be avoiding her gaze, when he responded. "I saw all those clocks in your room. If those can't get you out of bed, nothing I can do will budge you."

Audrey's heart slowed, then practically came to a halt. "You're not staying?"

"Oh, sweetheart, don't look like that," he whispered, cupping her face in his strong, gentle hands. "It's not because I don't want to be with you. I just don't want to put you under any more pressure. Let's give this some more time. I want you to be sure that it's really me you want and not the challenge I represent. I want you to trust me."

"But I do," she protested.

"Not enough. A part of you still fears I'm

going to control you. That's why you were so afraid to let go tonight. I think you felt you'd be losing yourself to me. I have to convince you that will never happen. I love the woman you are, including those traits that you see as weakness. I see them as compassion and generosity."

She shook her head. "There's a very fine line between giving and being taken advantage of. I learned that the hard way."

"Let me ask you this. When you do something for a friend does it make you feel good inside, whether you get something back or not?"

"Yes, of course."

"Then it couldn't be so wrong, could it? When you did things for this Derek, what was your motivation?"

"To show him how much I loved him."

"Then what was so terrible about that?"

"He hated me for it. He thought I was weak. He wanted somebody stronger."

Blake winced at her bitterness. "He was a fool. Loving someone, caring what happens to them, being generous with your time and your affection and asking nothing in return makes you a very special person. There are always going to be users in the world, people who'll take advantage of someone like you. They're the ones who need to be ashamed, not you.''

''Intellectually I know you're right, but I felt so used, so incredibly stupid.''

''You were used, but you were never stupid. It happens to a lot of people. You were merely blinded by love. You couldn't see that Derek was taking everything and giving nothing back. For some reason people like that always wind up resenting the person they've abused. As long as they're around, it's a reminder of their own faults.''

She stared at Blake in bewilderment, then dawning understanding. It was as though the film of confusion and hurt had been stripped away, leaving clarity for the first time, clarity and a sense of peace. ''Are you saying that Derek left me because I made him see himself too clearly?''

''Something like that.''

''Why couldn't I see that before?''

''Time and distance. You were too busy believing all those things he said about you to stop and wonder why he said them. That's another reason we need to take our time. I want you to know the kind of man I am. I will never take advantage of you, but my saying it isn't enough. I have to prove it to you."

"And you think you can do that?"

"I know it. I'm going to start by depositing you at the door of your room with a chaste kiss on the cheek and then I'm going back to my room and take a very cold shower."

"What happened to that togetherness shower you promised me?"

He grinned at her. "Keep it in mind. Anticipation is a wonderful thing."

Anticipation—she had another word for it— kept her awake all night. For the first time in her life, Audrey had no difficulty waking at dawn. She was actually humming as she drove to the rodeo grounds.

It was John Harley who spotted her first. "Hey, missy. I was afraid we might have scared you off after what happened on Friday. It's great to see you back."

"Thanks."

Blake looked up at John's greeting and smiled, his eyes filling with warmth. Then, he bent back over the propane tanks and went back to work without a word. A shiver of uneasiness slid down her spine. The look in his eyes had been welcoming, but then he'd seemed so distant, as though last night had never happened.

"Is there anything I can do to help?" she offered.

Harvey, out of breath and puffing, came hurrying up just in time to hear the question. He linked his hand through her elbow. "You can come with me."

She dug in her heels. "I'm on vacation."

He glowered at her. "I'm not asking, Audrey. I'm telling you. Come with me." She looked toward Blake, but he was pointedly ignoring the scene.

She whirled around and stomped off. "Damn you, Harvey, this better be important."

"Cool your heels, woman. I'm just trying to protect you. A reporter from one of those tabloids has been sneaking around town all night trying to pick up a line on you. If you're out there with Blake now, it'll be a dead giveaway and you'll be on the front page of that rag in every supermarket checkout line across America."

She groaned. "Does Blake know about this?"

"Of course. We've been trying to send the guy off on a wild-goose chase all morning, but the kid's tenacious as hell. As long as you stick with me so I can say you're just here as a member of the public relations staff, he might not make the connection.''

"What connection is that?'' a voice inquired from just behind Harvey. She could practically see the guy's smirk. "Is this the young lady everyone's been talking about?''

Harvey shot her a warning glance before plastering a jovial smile on his face and turning around. "Well, if it isn't Jake Brunetti again. How's the investigative reporting going?''

"Oh, I think I'm on to something now,'' the man said, his knowing gaze traveling over Audrey in a way that made her feel as though she ought to go take another shower. "This wouldn't happen to be the young woman everyone on Marshall's team is so busy protecting?''

"I don't need any protection, Mr. Brunetti,'' she said very, very quietly. The minute Harvey had mentioned the man's name she'd realized what they were up against. Jake Brunetti had a lot of big stories with tantalizing headlines. He got his information without much regard for ethics. "What about you? Are your lawyers still getting rich from your libel suits?''

She could practically feel Harvey tensing beside her. She was sure it he'd had a clear shot he'd have kicked her for taunting the man. She took a deep breath and tried to cool her temper.

"Sharp tongue," Brunetti noted with a man-to-man glance at Harvey. "I can see why Marshall would want a piece of that action."

"Why you..." Harvey had drawn back a fist and the only thing that kept it from connecting with Brunetti's pug nose was Audrey's iron-clad grip on his forearm.

"Would you care for a tip, Mr. Brunetti?" she said sweetly. He was too stupid to realize that her change in attitude was abrupt and insincere. "I've heard that the woman you're looking for left for the airport at dawn. I think Mr. Marshall plans to have her flown out of here in his private jet. He mentioned something about Las Vegas. You might want to check it out. Perhaps that's where they're having the wedding."

Jake Brunetti's eyes lit up and he was practically licking his lips at the prospect of an international scoop. "You're sure about this?"

"Well, as sure as you can be with anything to do with Mr. Marshall," she said with a little you-know-how-it-is shrug. "He's a man who makes up his mind in a hurry and changes it just as quickly. We never quite know what to expect."

"You know him, then?"

"I work for him."

"Thanks for the tip, lady." He scowled at
Harvey. "You ought to take a few lessons from
her, Fielding. Cooperating with the press is a
good policy. If you treat us right, we'll do the
same for you."

Audrey managed to contain her laughter until
Brunetti was out of earshot. Then she and Harvey both started chuckling. "Very nice," Harvey congratulated her. "Just one thing. What
happens when he gets to the airport and finds
that the plane is still on the ground?"

She widened her eyes innocently. "Is that
what he's going to find?"

Harvey's laughter boomed through the morning air. "Right. I'll go call the pilot right now.
He ought to be able to file a flight plan and hide
the plane before the boy reporter can check it
out."

"Now can I go back and wish Blake luck?"

"Be my guest."

She found Blake in the gondola offering tether
rides to anyone willing to make a contribution
to Mountain Rescue. A long line, mostly gig-
gling teenagers and eager women, was queued
up awaiting a turn. The minute he saw her,

though, he landed the balloon and motioned her over.

He leaned down and whispered in her ear, "Everything okay with Harvey?"

"He's doing just fine. He's busy making sure that the reporter will head for Las Vegas to try to pin down when and where you'll be married."

"Not bad," he said, his eyes lighting up. "Is there any truth to the rumor?"

"Why, Mr. Marshall, only you can answer that."

"I don't think it's a bad idea, but I would need a bride."

She gestured at the line. "There seem to be plenty of ladies here who'd probably volunteer."

"I'm only interested in one particular lady."

"I will get married in a Las Vegas chapel when pigs fly," she said. Blake chuckled at her adamant tone.

"I'll have to come up with a better plan, then."

"You certainly will."

"Are you going to fly with me today?"

"I think one test of my courage in a weekend

is more than enough, thank you. You have a good flight and win this thing, okay?''

"I'll do my best."

Audrey brushed a kiss across his lips and patted him on the cheek. "Just try to keep your mind on what you're doing this time," she said.

Blake scowled at her with feigned ferocity, as John hooted and the rest of the crew pointedly turned away to hide their laughter. "Why you little…"

"Careful, boss," John cautioned with a dry chuckle. "I think you've finally met your match."

Blake's eyes glinted with admiration as Audrey turned around and winked at him audaciously.

He shook his head at that and grinned. "I think you may be right."

Twelve

When Audrey got back to the shelter, Harvey was raking his fingers frantically through his hair. Little tufts were standing up every which way. At the sight of her, an expression of relief washed over his face.

"Thank God, you're here. I was just going to come looking for you. Something terrible's happened. We have to do something." His words were running together in a nervous rush.

Audrey's heartbeat slowed. She'd never, ever seen Harvey this agitated before. Excited, yes. But never uncertain. He was usually calm, totally unflappable. She was almost afraid to say anything for fear he'd fall apart completely.

"What?" she said at last. "What's wrong, Harvey?"

"It's Kelly Marie!"

There were actually tears in his eyes and she felt a sinking sensation in the pit of her stomach. "Oh, no! Not the baby." She grabbed Harvey's arm. "Has something gone wrong? She hasn't lost the baby, has she?"

"Not yet, but she's gone into premature labor. Joe's an absolute mess. He just called. He's all alone back there, no family nearby."

"I thought Kelly Marie's mother was with them."

"I did, too, but apparently she had to go home yesterday and can't get back right away. I'm worried sick about the poor kid. You should have heard him. What the hell do you do in a situation like this? You're a woman. You should know what to do."

"Calm, down, Harvey," she soothed, trying to think rationally in the face of Harvey's unexpected hysteria. "You go on back to California. Be there for Joe. Blake will understand. I can wrap things up here. There's not that much left to do anyway."

Harvey looked at her as though she'd suggested he take up skydiving. "Uh-uh. Not me. I can't go. I won't know what to do. Joe will end up reassuring me."

She was beginning to see the truth of that. In some ways, she found it endearing, a sign of the depth of his caring. "All he needs is a shoulder to lean on," she told him. "Just be a friend."

"But I'm no good at this stuff. I fainted in the delivery room every time one of my kids was born."

She restrained a grin. "Harvey, you won't have to be in the delivery room. I promise."

He squinted at her distrustfully and shook his head. "Audrey, I'm telling you Joe needs somebody who can handle a crisis."

She could see there was no arguing him out of it. Without another instant's hesitation she said, "Okay, then I'll go. You make the arrangements and I'll get back to the motel and pack. Do you think Blake's pilot would be able to fly me back?"

Now that he had specific, familiar things to do, Harvey was back in control. "No problem. I'll take care of everything. You just get yourself to the airport. I'll have the pilot waiting. He should be out there already since I asked him to file that fake flight plan to throw off Brunetti. Call me as soon as you get to the hospital and let me know what's happening. If Joe phones again, I'll tell him you're on your way.''

It wasn't until she was in the air and caught sight of the balloons down below that Audrey realized she hadn't left a message for Blake telling him what had happened. Surely, though, Harvey would take care of it. At the very least, he'd have to explain to Blake why his plane was missing.

Exhausted by the tensions of the past few days, along with the long hours and unaccustomed activity, Audrey promptly fell asleep. When she awoke, the pilot was standing over her and they were on the ground in California.

''Miss Nelson, there's a driver waiting for you. Mr. Fielding said he was to take you straight to the hospital. Is that okay?''

''That's fine, thanks. And thank you for the smooth ride.''

He grinned at her. ''I'm glad you were able to sleep through the storm.''

''Storm?'' A shiver raced down her spine.

''It was pretty bumpy for a while, but I maneuvered around the worst of it. It took us a little longer that way, but it was safer.''

"I must have been even more exhausted than I realized," she muttered gratefully as she hurried down the steps and into the waiting car.

When she reached the hospital, she found Joe even more frazzled than Harvey had been. He had dark circles under his eyes and a pile of discarded candy wrappers was on the table next to him. He was staring blankly up at the ceiling.

"Having a chocolate attack?" she murmured lightly. He glanced at her and gave her a faint smile that came and went in an instant.

"Thanks for coming."

She sat down next to him and reached over to touch his tightly clenched hands. "How's it going?"

His fingers relaxed long enough to clasp hers in a painful grip. "They took Kelly Marie into the operating room a little while ago. They're doing a Caesarean."

"Have they told you anything?"

"They said the baby might not make it because it's so early."

Audrey closed her eyes, then forced herself to meet Joe's gaze. "You're not going to give up hope, do you hear me. This baby is going to be just fine. Lots of babies are premature and make it."

"God, I hope so. Kelly Marie will never forgive herself if we lose the baby. That's all she's been able to talk about for the past week, ever since the trouble started. She thinks she must have done something wrong."

"No matter what happens, she'll be okay as long as she knows you don't blame her. The two of you can get through anything, as long as you stick together."

With nothing left to say, Audrey fell silent. The pile of candy wrappers grew. It seemed an eternity before a weary-looking doctor, still wearing his green scrub uniform, came into the waiting room. Joe's eyes widened with fear.

"Doctor?" he said hesitantly.

"You have a son."

"He's okay?" Joe whispered, as though he hardly dared to hope for a miracle.

"So far," the doctor said with a tired smile. "He weighs two and a half pounds and we've pulled them through smaller than that. I have every expectation he'll make it."

Joe pumped the man's hand gratefully. "And Kelly Marie, can I see her?"

"She's still pretty out of it. Why don't you go home and get some sleep."

Audrey could see the mutinous expression

forming on Joe's lips and said, "Wouldn't it be okay if he just peeked in on her for a minute?"

The doctor smiled. "I don't suppose it would hurt. Just don't stay long. She's had a rough time of it."

"And the baby?"

"Go down to the ICU and tell the nurse who you are. She'll let you get a look at him." He put a hand on Joe's shoulder. "Let me warn you about something, though. He's in an isolette and there are a lot of tubes and wires. It horrifies some parents at first. Please, try not to let it upset you. Remember it's all there to give him the best possible chance to make it. If you think of it that way, maybe it won't seem so cruel."

Audrey went with Joe to Kelly Marie's room and waited outside while he saw her. Then they walked to the newborn intensive care unit. The nurse showed them how to gown up, then led them to the isolette.

"He's so tiny," Joe breathed.

Audrey had to swallow the lump that formed in her throat at the sight of the baby overwhelmed by all that equipment. "But you heard the doctor," she said. "He's got every chance of pulling through. You hang on to that."

They only stayed for a few minutes and when

they were back in the hall, Joe said, "Audrey, thank you again for coming back tonight. I don't know what I would have done without you. I'm just so sorry about your vacation and everything."

"Don't worry about it. This is what friends are for. You just promise me that I'll be on the top of the list of baby-sitters."

"You've got it. Now, come on and I'll drive you home."

It took twenty minutes for Joe to take her to her apartment, which seemed even lonelier than usual with middle-of-the-night shadows filling the corners. She tried to picture Blake lounging on the sofa or sitting at her desk. Even though he'd never been in her apartment, she found it was incredibly easy to envision him there. The image brought a smile to her lips. She wondered what it would be like to have him as a husband. Would he be there for her as Joe had been for Kelly Marie? She was sure of it. There was an reassuring aura of constancy and stability underlying his facade of recklessness.

Enough of this, she thought. She tried to put Blake, Joe and Kelly Marie out of her mind, but it took a warm bath and an hour of reading for her to unwind enough to go to bed. She had barely closed her eyes, when the phone rang.

Dear God, she prayed, not the baby!

"Hello." Her voice was tentative.

"Where the devil have you been?"

It was Blake and, if it hadn't been for his impatient tone, she might have been very glad to hear from him. As it was, she immediately went on the defensive. Before she could open her mouth to tell him off, though, he hit her with another barrage of shouted, ill-tempered questions.

"Do you have any idea how worried I've been? What got into you just taking off like that without a word? I've been frantic. Couldn't you at least have left some explanation, a note, anything?"

"I wasn't aware that I was accountable to you," she said.

"You are if you're going to go flying off in my plane."

"Is that what you're upset about? Because I borrowed you plane?"

Blake sighed. "Don't be ridiculous. You know damn well it's more than that. I thought you were someone I could count on."

"I beg your pardon," Audrey said, her tone

ominous. "Are you implying that I'm not reliable?"

"You heard me. For the second day in a row I'm sitting in an empty hotel room, trying to figure out where the hell you've disappeared to. I thought we had an understanding. I expected you to be here when the race was over."

"And I would have been if something hadn't come up."

"Something more important than us?"

"Yes, in this instance, it was." Her voice was cool, but she was seething inside at Blake's quick judgment, his attempt to pit their relationship against the very real needs of a friend. Blake was the man who'd said caring for friends was important. Apparently that only counted when it didn't inconvenience him. "For your information, I flew back because Kelly Marie nearly lost the baby last night and Joe needed me here. Now, if you don't mind, I am very tired and I think I'd better hang up before we both say some things we're going to regret."

"Audrey, dammit..."

She didn't wait to see if he minded. She slammed the phone down in his ear. It took less than thirty seconds for it to ring again. She yanked the plug out of the wall. When she could still hear the extension ringing in the living room, she buried her head under the pillow. Finally it stopped.

Furious and wide awake now, she lay on her back and stared at the ceiling. Of all the arrogant, overbearing, pompous, selfish... She finally ran out of adjectives suitable for describing what she thought of Blake's attitude. How could she have been so stupid? She had honestly believed all that stuff he'd said about admiring her loyalty and generosity. Sure he admired it. As long as it didn't disrupt his plans. Well, she'd be damned if she was going to feel guilty for coming back here to help out a friend.

She was still seething three hours later, when the pounding started at the front door. Recalling the broken door on her motel room back in Aspen, she jumped out of bed and threw on her robe as she hurried into the living room.

"Don't you dare break down my door," she shouted as she flung it open, just in time to see a blur as Blake stormed past. She glared at him. He glowered back.

"I wouldn't have had to touch the door, if you'd answered your phone."

"There was no one I cared to talk to."

"Fine. Then you can listen to me."

Bare toes curled into the carpet and she clenched her fists at her sides in a losing fight for control. Finally, she snapped, "Not on your life, buster."

Hands on hips she faced him down. "If you think you can call up here and berate me for caring about a friend, then you've got another think coming. I'm terribly sorry, if you were worried, but did it ever occur to you to ask Harvey where I'd gone? I assumed he'd tell you, especially since I took your plane, but you probably just barged into the motel room again, blew your top and took off like a crazy man."

She thought she caught a flicker of guilt in the depths of his eyes. He was either toying with an apology or an explosion. She forestalled either one, by plunging on, "Maybe I should have left a note, but I had this crazy idea you'd understand. I thought getting back here to help Joe out in a real crisis was more important than worrying about whether or not you might get a little miffed when you couldn't find me."

"*A little miffed!* Is that what you think this is all about? I was worried sick about you. After the story broke in the paper…"

Audrey looked at him in confusion. "What story?"

"The one about us. Jake Brunetti apparently did some adding without his calculator. He strung together a few facts into a torrid little affair. I'm sure you'll be able to catch it next time you shop for groceries."

"Oh, hell."

"Indeed." There was a wry tone to his voice. "I thought it might have frightened you off. Harvey was already on a commercial flight back by the time I started looking for him. When my pilot said he'd flown you back here earlier, I was convinced you'd decided that you and I were through. It would be just like you to go off in my plane just to make a statement."

She waved aside his fears with a gesture of incredulity. "Because of a little publicity? I'm tougher than that and I don't go around stealing planes. I merely borrowed it for a few hours. Obviously you got it back, since you're here now."

"All right. We'll forget about the plane. And I know how tough you are. I wasn't sure you did. It still astonishes me how a woman with your temper could ever have imagined herself as weak. And I'm sorry for coming down on you so hard." He hesitated. "I was scared," he finally admitted softly. "That's all."

Audrey stared at him in surprise. "Scared? You?"

"I don't want to lose you. Don't you know that by now?"

"You aren't going to lose me that easily."

Their eyes clashed, but neither of them moved to close the distance between them.

"Now what's all this about Kelly Marie?" Blake asked. "Is she okay?"

The tenor of the conversation had switched so fast, Audrey's head was reeling. "She's fine and the baby should make it."

"She had the baby?"

"A boy. He's tiny, but he's fighting."

Blake held out his arms, but Audrey waited. "I'm glad you were here for Joe," he said softly and then she moved into his embrace. "Really."

"Me, too," she said, her voice muffled against Blake's chest. Having his arms around her made her feel astonishingly safe and secure. In some ways that worried her, but mostly it reassured her. "Joe needed someone. It was a very frightening experience."

His arms held her more tightly. "I need someone, too."

"I could call Harvey," she suggested lightly.

"He's not the person I had in mind."

"Who, then?"

"You." He breathed a heavy sigh. "You have no idea how I felt when I thought I might have lost you." His lips touched hers hungrily, before moving on to the pulse at the base of her throat.

"The race, Blake," she said breathlessly. "What happened?"

"I don't want to talk about the race." He slipped her robe off one shoulder and blazed a trail of kisses along the bare flesh, setting off fireworks.

"Then you must have won," she said with confidence.

"Actually, I lost. Now would you be quiet for a minute." He did his best to silence her with another breath-stealing kiss. The robe fell away and she stood before him in the muted light, naked once again, but no longer vulnerable. This time she felt totally sure of herself. More important, she felt sure of Blake. If there were decisions to be made, her heart seemed to have made them for her.

"You are so incredibly lovely," he whispered. "How did I ever get to be so lucky?"

The heat in Blake's eyes told her he desired her, but more than that, his voice told her of his love. She wanted to share that love in the most important way possible between a man and a woman. She wanted it now, before she lost her courage.

"And you have far too many clothes on," she said softly, reaching for the buttons on his shirt. When the shirt fell open, she raked her nails along his bare chest, feeling the tensing of his muscles as she reached the waistband of his pants. Her fingers fumbled with his belt buckle and when it was free, she moved on, the teasing torment making his breathing ragged. The soft rasp of his zipper sent a shiver racing down her spine.

Then Blake's impatient fingers replaced hers and his clothes were stripped away. They flew in all directions with untidy abandon. Anxious arms pulled her tight against him, the heat of their flesh setting off a wild pounding of her heart. His warm, musky scent was intoxicating. And at the hard thrust of his manhood against the softness of her inner thigh, Audrey felt a stirring of incredible excitement. She moved to readjust her position to an even more intimate one, but Blake stilled her.

"Slowly, love. This time we're going to take it very slowly and enjoy every sweet second of it."

As he spoke, his eyes were bold in their survey, then smoky with a provocative sensuality. He kissed her throat, her shoulders and then circled her nipples with his tongue until they were full and throbbing. His deft fingers massaged slowly, then swept over bare flesh with lightning speed creating a pattern of exquisite torture that set her blood on fire and filled her with an urgent, desperate longing.

Audrey's gaze never left Blake's face, searching his eyes for the intensity of feeling that matched her own. When at long last he held out his hand, she took it without hesitation. The walk to the bedroom had never seemed longer, her knees never weaker, her pulse never faster. At the sight of her bed, its sheets still rumpled from her tossing and turning, Blake's patience and incredible willpower failed him at last. He scooped her into his arms and knelt with her on the edge of the bed. When she nipped at a masculine nipple, a violent shudder ripped through him and they suddenly tumbled onto the bed in a tangle of arms and legs, laughing at themselves and their haste.

Then Blake's kisses were everywhere, his touch so intimate that at first she was shocked, then thrilled by the wildness of the sensations.

As the play of his fingers went on, tension coiled within her, tightening to an unbearable level of excitement. If this was anticipation as Blake meant it always to be, she would live for the joy of it. She saw the peak just ahead, felt its pull and knew an instant's fear that this time would be like before, that instead of a shattering explosion, there would be only a slow descent, then nothing.

But Blake gave her no time to dwell on the fear and allow it to become panic. His caresses were insistent, a slow, sweet torture that never once let up until she was twisting and turning, arching toward fingers that seemed possessed of the devil because they stirred such incredible feelings in her.

"Hold me, Blake. I need you with me."

"Not yet, sweetheart. This time is just for you."

His tongue found the moist heat at her core and set off a violent trembling. Her muscles tensed, fighting against going on alone, but then with another flick of Blake's tongue, she was free, spinning out of control, great waves washing over her.

Her body, glistening with a sheen of perspiration, stilled slowly, and she was filled with a sensation of such incredible joy that she thought it might never be matched again no matter how many times Blake held her in his arms. Blake had taken her to the heights, overcome her fears and taught her to fly again. He had given her back the ability to love and with tears rolling down her cheeks, she embraced him.

"That was the most wonderful gift any man has ever given a woman," she murmured. "Thank you."

"We're not finished yet," he said, his mouth seeking her breast.

To her delight and astonishment, ripples of excitement began all over again, building with even greater intensity. When Blake joined her at last, she felt complete and they moved together in the timeless, perfect rhythm of eternal lovers. Together, they traveled farther and faster to a world beyond her previous imagination, a world of bright colors, spectacular sounds and incomparably intense sensations.

Together, they found a little piece of heaven right here on earth.

When their moment out of time ended and the real world invaded their sense of isolation, Blake felt utterly at peace. He had seen the future and Audrey was there. All that remained was to con-

vince her of that. He saw the joy and contentment on her face and thought the time was right.

"We have plans to make," he said.

"What plans?" she muttered sleepily.

"Don't fade out on me here. I know you're
not good in the morning, but I thought that only
counted when you'd been asleep."

"If I'm incoherent now, it's because of you.
What exactly is it you want to discuss?"

"Our wedding, unless of course you're prepared to have it in one of those awful Las Vegas
chapels with strangers around and a rental bouquet. It would make Jake Brunetti very happy to
be proved right, of course."

"Don't you think you're being a little impul-
sive? We hardly know each other."

"I don't think that's true. You learn a lot
about a person when you're stranded together."

"We were hardly lost in the jungle for weeks
on end."

"There were dangers," he countered. "Have
you forgotten the lightning?"

"Hardly, but suppose I accept your theory. In
a time of danger emotions are also heightened.
You can't trust them."

"I do. I know what I feel for you, but if you
need to wait awhile, I'll go through the whole

courtship routine. We'll just be postponing the inevitable, though. Sometimes fate takes matters into its own hands.''

''I don't think fate had anything to do with hauling me into that balloon.''

''Whatever.''

''Besides, I thought you were convinced I needed time to trust you, to really know the kind of man you are.''

''That's true,'' he said agreeably. ''I just don't see any reason why you can't figure all that out after we're married, say over the next fifty years or so.''

Suddenly Audrey was out of his arms, kneeling beside him. She grabbed a pillow and began hitting him with it. ''Blast you, Blake Marshall!''

''What did I do now?'' he said, laughing as he tried to ward off the ineffectual blows. For all her pretense of fury, he sensed she wasn't really angry, only frustrated. He could hardly wait to hear why.

''You have made it virtually impossible for me to say no.''

''That was the idea,'' he said, ducking another swing.

"But I made a promise to myself in Aspen that I was going to start saying no."

He studied her in bemusement. "Let me see if I understand this. You're admitting that you love me and that you want to marry me?"

"Right."

"But you can't say yes."

"Exactly."

He shrugged. "No problem."

"No problem?"

"Say no, if that's what you feel you have to do," he said, trying not to chuckle at her suddenly crestfallen expression.

"You don't really care?"

"Not as long as what you mean is yes."

She eyed him warily. "There's a trick here, isn't there?"

"Not as far as I can tell," he said innocently. "So, what is it? Will you marry me?"

She grinned and fell on top of him. "No." Her arms crept around his neck. "No." Her lips seared his bare shoulder. "No."

Before he gave himself up to the sensations, he murmured, "Be sure and let me know when you've set the date."

* * * * *

SILHOUETTE *Romance*™

Escape to a place where a kiss is still a kiss...
Feel the breathless connection...
Fall in love as though it were
the very first time...
Experience the power of love!

Come to where favorite authors—such as
Diana Palmer, Stella Bagwell,
Marie Ferrarella and many more—
deliver heart-warming romance and genuine
emotion, time after time after time....

Silhouette Romance—
stories straight from the heart!

Silhouette®
Where love comes alive™

Visit Silhouette at www.eHarlequin.com.   SRDIR1

INTIMATE MOMENTS™
Romance, Adventure—Excitement

IF YOU'VE GOT THE TIME... WE'VE GOT THE INTIMATE MOMENTS

Passion. Suspense. Desire. Drama.
Enter a world that's larger
than life, where men and women
overcome life's greatest odds
for the ultimate prize: love.
Nonstop excitement is closer
than you think...in
Silhouette Intimate Moments!

Silhouette®
Where love comes alive™

Visit Silhouette at www.eHarlequin.com

SIMDIR1

passionate powerful provocative love stories that fulfill your every desire

Silhouette Desire delivers strong heroes, spirited
heroines and stellar love stories.

Desire features your favorite authors, including

Diana Palmer, Annette Broadrick, Ann Major, Anne MacAllister and Cait London.

Passionate, powerful and provocative
romances *guaranteed!*

For superlative authors, sensual stories and
sexy heroes, choose Silhouette Desire.

Available at your favorite retail outlet.

Where love comes alive™

passionate powerful provocative love stories that fulfill your every desire

Visit us at www.eHarlequin.com   SDGEN00

V *Silhouette*

SPECIAL EDITION™

Emotional, compelling stories that capture the intensity of living, loving and creating a family in today's world.

Special Edition features bestselling authors such as Nora Roberts, Diana Palmer, Sherryl Woods, Lindsay McKenna, Joan Elliott Pickart— and many more!

For a romantic, complex and emotional read, choose Silhouette Special Edition.

Available at your favorite retail outlet.

Where love comes alive™

Visit Silhouette at www.eHarlequin.com

SSEGEN00

♥ *Silhouette*®

SPECIAL EDITION™

Emotional, compelling stories that
capture the intensity of living,
loving and creating a family
in today's world.

♥ *Silhouette*®

Desire

A highly passionate,
emotionally powerful and
always provocative
read.

♥ *Silhouette*®

Where love comes alive™

♥ *Silhouette*

INTIMATE MOMENTS™

A roller-coaster read that delivers
romantic thrills in a world of
suspense, adventure
and more.

SILHOUETTE *Romance*

From first love to forever,
these love stories are for
today's woman with
traditional values.

Visit Silhouette at www.eHarlequin.com

SILGENINT

Where love comes alive™

From first love to forever, these love stories are
for today's woman with traditional values.

A highly passionate, emotionally powerful
and always provocative read.

SPECIAL EDITION™

Emotional, compelling stories that capture the
intensity of living, loving and creating a family in
today's world.

Silhouette®

INTIMATE MOMENTS™

A roller-coaster read that delivers romantic thrills
in a world of suspense, adventure and more.

Visit Silhouette at www.eHarlequin.com

SDIR2